A BOOK TO DIE FOR

A COSTA RICA COZY MYSTERY #2

K.C. AMES

17th STREET BOOKS

ABOUT THIS BOOK

New bookstore, new dead body!

Days away from the grand opening of her new bookstore, Dana Kirkpatrick couldn't be more excited, until her excitement turns to horror when she discovers a dead body between the bookshelves.

Now Dana must find the killer, protect a valuable book collection, and hopefully, open her store as planned while her own life is in danger.

Can the San Francisco transplant solve the case and open her bookstore before anyone else dies?

Although this is a series the books stand alone and you can read them in any order you like.

AUTHOR'S NOTE

Hello and welcome!

If you love exotic animals, beaches, and good food then I'm pretty sure you're going to enjoy the fun ride ahead.

A Book To Die For is the second book of my Costa Rica Beach Cozy Mystery Series. There are many more adventures to come, so make sure you sign up for my newsletter so I can keep you in the know.

And by signing up you'll have access to a lot of cool stuff including my **Costa Rica Recipe Book**, free!

Subscribers will also have access to my personal pictures of some of the exotic animals I've encountered in Costa Rica (like sloths and monkeys) and pictures of my fearsome threesome (my Cavalier King Charles, Havanese, and Chihuahua).

https://kcames.com/subscribe/

ONE

After months of preparation, and a lot of the proverbial sweat, blood, and tears, the grand opening of Dana Kirkpatrick's bookstore was two days away, but there was still a lot to do before then, so she woke up earlier than usual to tackle her never-ending to-do list as soon as possible.

At five a.m. her iPhone alarm blasted a Luscious Jackson song, waking her and Wally up.

Wally was Dana's cat, who had been sleeping at the bottom of the bed, curled up against her legs. Dana yawned and sat up, looking down at the kitty that looked back at her with just one eye open. She laughed at his *what do you think you're doing this early* look he gave her.

"Good morning," she said to the cat.

Wally was not amused with her early morning cheeriness. Dana could almost swear that if he weren't so comatose, he would have hissed back.

"Hey, don't give me that 'tude, I have a lot of stuff to do today. Grand opening is a few days away."

Wally plopped his tiny head back onto the bed. He yawned

and stretched while lying on his side. She wouldn't get any help from him.

"Bum," Dana said as she got out of bed.

To her surprise, Wally got up. "Oh, you are going to help? Good, because you need to get some practice at being the bookstore cat."

Wally yawned for what must have been the fifth time, but he tossed in a downward-facing dog yoga pose at the same time, then he moseyed up to where Dana had been sleeping and plopped down on the warm spot she had left behind, promptly going back to sleep.

"Or not," Dana said, chuckling as she made her way to the bathroom.

She brushed her teeth, washed her face, and quickly got dressed. She glanced over at the bed as she slipped on her Rothy's slip-on flat shoes, perfect for the busy day she had in front of her.

Wally was fast asleep again and didn't even bother to look up at her as she made her way out of the room. She gave him one more look over her shoulder. He was out cold.

"Bum," she said again, making her way downstairs to the kitchen.

It was 5:12 a.m. She grabbed a bag of fresh coffee beans from her friend Mindy's family farm in the Tarrazú region.

The beans had just been packed up a few days ago. *It doesn't get fresher than this*, Dana thought as she dumped a few spoonfuls of the delicious-smelling beans into a bean grinder. She hit the button, and the machine began to whirl and buzz as it ground up the beans.

She added water to the coffeemaker while the bean grinder did its thing. When the machine stopped making its racket, she took the container of freshly ground coffee and she put her nose in there like she was sniffing fine wine and took a deep inhale.

Smells so good, she thought as she dumped the freshly ground coffee into the coffeemaker and hit the brew button—something she had done so often that the text spelling "brew" on the button had long ago rubbed off.

While the coffee brewed, she ate a bowl of dry cereal and a banana handpicked from her backyard.

Less than ten minutes later, with a large coffee tumbler in hand, she climbed into Big Red—the nickname she had given to her cherry-red vintage 1948 Jeep Willys, which was parked in the carport.

She fired Big Red up and she made the quick drive from her place to Ark Row on Main Street, where all the retail stores in town were located and where her soon-to-open bookstore would join the ark row.

It was about 5:35 a.m. and still pitch-dark out when she parked in front. She had a heavy box of books that she had packed up the day before in the backseat, so she would have to come back for the coffee tumbler full of that precious life-giving liquid.

She grabbed the box, struggling to get a good grip on it. It was heavy, but she got a good hold of it as she made her way to her locked store.

At the front door, she hoisted the box onto a bent knee as she fidgeted around in her bag for the store's keys, which seemed to think it would be fun to play a game of hide-and-seek as she tried to balance the heavy box on one knee.

"Dang it," she said, giving up the balancing act. She plopped the heavy box on the floor by her feet so she could focus on finding the elusive key.

"There you are, you little stinker," she said out loud into her purse as she pulled out the key.

She unlocked the upward-coiling security grille that restricted access to the front door and pushed it up until it rolled up into a tube. Now she had access to the front door, which she unlocked. She turned on the lights then went back outside and picked up the box of books and hoisted it onto the counter.

She felt a strange energy that made the tiny brown hairs on her arm stand at attention. She shrugged it off. It was early in the morning—dark and quiet, which caused the brain to interpret it as an ominous vibe.

"What you need is coffee," she said out loud to herself. She began to head to the door in order to go fetch her coffee tumbler from the Jeep, but that creepy vibe niggled at the back of her mind as she walked, so she looked over her shoulder towards the counter and froze.

Did I just see what I saw?

She turned around to be sure, taking a few steps towards the counter, trying to convince herself that it was the darkness or the sleep in her eyes messing with her, making her see things that weren't there.

Too bad it wasn't just her mind playing tricks on her.

She wanted to scream but couldn't. She wanted to run outside but couldn't. Her feet felt like they were encased in two buckets of hardened cement.

She stood there for what seemed to be hours, but was just a moment or two as she stared down at the floor, at the two feet sticking out from the other side of the counter.

Finally, her body released her mind from its stupor and she ran outside, screaming.

TWO

Three months earlier—before she found a dead body inside her bookstore—Dana had stood in the center of that very spot which had been an empty retail store for years and known it was the perfect spot for her bookstore.

It was her third visit, but she knew the moment she had walked inside the first time that she was standing in her future bookstore, which she already planned to call Mariposa Books.

Luis Padilla, her spryly real estate agent, who was in his late twenties, stepped outside to take a call, so she was able to stand there by herself in silence, taking in the open space and visualizing her bookstore.

"Talk to me," she said to the open space. She closed her eyes for a moment then opened them and quickly looked back to make sure she was still alone.

That would have been embarrassing, she thought as she confirmed that Padilla was still outside gabbing on his phone working on another deal.

Dana smiled, figuring that if he had been there, he would have just shrugged off her talking to an empty room as the California hippy-dippy thing to do.

Dana went back to the task at hand as she walked around the entire space, *again*.

She looked at everything, from the floorboards to the ceiling. She inspected every nook and cranny.

It was a great location, smack in the middle of Ark Row on Main Street.

Ark Row was the nickname given to the retail center of Mariposa Beach that consisted of several stand-alone cottages side-by-side. Long ago those cottages had been boats that served as residential homes that were anchored out in the water, year-round; because they were houseboats on the water with arched roofs, decks, and French doors they were referred to as arks.

In the 1960s, the government put a kibosh on the anchored-out arks, so the houseboats were brought to shore, eventually becoming the retail location known as Ark Row.

The original merchants saw the branding power of Ark Row, so when new retail buildings were built, they convinced the municipality to make it a requirement that the developers keep the look and feel of the original arks, and that is how Ark Row came to be.

Even Main Street was more of a marketing tool than any, since it was the only thoroughfare in town anyway, so the locals jokingly called it Only Street.

Mariposa Beach didn't have any traffic lights, and the one stop sign in town was treated as a yield sign, much to the frightening realization of tourists walking down or driving on Only Street.

But to the Ark Row merchants, the connotations of Main Street, USA was a powerful marketing tool that they had embraced wholeheartedly.

None of that mattered to Dana back then as she just stood in the middle of an empty retail space, taking stock of everything and getting excited at the prospect of opening her book-store there.

There was also the voice of fear rattling in her head, reminding her of the fact that she stood inside the empty store-front of an out-of-business store, a reminder of the risks of starting a new business, especially a bookstore—an endangered form of retail business that had been going the way of the dodo bird as just about everyone and their great-grandmother were getting into reading books digitally or ordering their print books online.

Dana was lost in those thoughts and in the silence and still-ness of the moment when suddenly she heard Luis Padilla's booming voice from behind her. "Perfect! Isn't it?" His voice bounced around the empty walls loud enough to make Dana jump.

"Sorry, I didn't mean to startle you."

Dana caught her breath. "It's okay. I didn't hear you come back in, and I was lost with my thoughts."

"I understand. You have a lot to think about, but as far as the location, this would be a perfect spot for your bookstore. It's right in the heart of Ark Row," Padilla said. Dana smiled. Like he had told her something she didn't know.

"It's a great location, there is no doubt about that," she finally replied, looking around at the space again.

"It was a thriving video store for like twenty years, even outlived Blockbuster by a few years," Padilla said, grinning. "It has a great layout for a bookstore. Instead of shelves of videos, it will have shelves of books. And look," he said, not letting her get a word in, "there is a lot of room for expansion. Like right over there," he said, pointing at an empty corner covered in dust, "you could put a little cafe there. Get people to come in for coffee, pastries... *books*," he said with an arched eyebrow.

Dana smiled. "Baby steps, Luis. I don't know the first thing about lattes and pastries, but I do know books."

She kept looking around and mulling it over in her head. He was right about the location. It was perfect for her needs. It was a much bigger space than she needed, but the price was a steal. But should she? Dana was doing it again. She second-guessed herself a few dozen times a day about starting her own business in a dying industry and in a country she had just moved down to a few months ago. She kept hearing her mom's voice in her head. *You're getting in over your head... you're getting in over your head.*

The experience of starting a new business would be new to her, but she had experience working in a dying business.

She graduated with a journalism degree from the University of California, Berkeley. She paid her dues working for smaller newspapers until she made it to her hometown newspaper, the *San Francisco Times.*

It wasn't the *New York Times* or even the *L.A. Times*, but it was the big leagues of print journalism, not that her pay reflected it.

It didn't help matters that digital media was eating print media's lunch.

The decline of the print newspaper business reminded Dana of that Buggel's song, "Video Killed the Radio Star," and how the Internet did just that to print media, and she had a front-row seat to the carnage.

It seemed that anyone with a blog—and later a Twitter, YouTube, or Facebook account—was a journalist, and old-school journalists were expected to not just report the news, but more importantly generate web content... a lot of content, which made it difficult to do a journalist job properly. Fact-checking and vetting sources took a backseat in favor of getting poorly vetted, short-word-count articles with a click-bait headline on the newspaper's website as soon as possible.

Dana figured that if her journalist background was going to be a hindrance to the business side of the newspaper business—who seemed to want bloggers, not journalists—and having grown tired of low morale, salary cutbacks and freezes, slashed budgets, and most of the resources siphoned to the online division of the newspaper, she might as well go make some money, for a change. So she left the *San Francisco Times* for a swanky public relations firm in the SoMa district of San Francisco.

"Penny for your thoughts?" Padilla's voice pulled Dana's mind back from those memories and to the empty retail store she was standing in.

"It could work," she replied to Padilla while inside she was asking herself, *Am I making a mistake?*

Yes, this is too risky, the right side of her brain replied.

No, you're not; go for it, the left part of her brain piped in.

It's not like she was making decisions based purely on emotion. She had done her homework since she left the hectic big-city life of San Francisco for the quiet, small, beach-town community of Mariposa Beach, Costa Rica, a town and country that relied heavily on tourism.

She also saw the instant and free inventory that landed on her lap as serendipity.

When she inherited her uncle's property, it included her uncle's huge collection of books. Boom. Instant inventory.

After some legal battles over the property, she now owned Casa Verde free and clear.

"So... what do you think?" Padilla asked again.

"I think I need coffee," she replied, seeing the frustration on his face.

She made her way outside, Padilla following her as he looked at his wristwatch. He oozed a "time is money" mantra with every step he took. "Okay, call me when you make up your mind and we'll get the paperwork started," he said as he got into his Toyota RAV4 SUV.

"I will," Dana said as she crossed the street, heading over to her friend Mindy's cafe.

"Were you visiting the store again?" Mindy asked Dana from behind the counter as soon as she walked in.

Dana smiled sheepishly and nodded. "Have to be sure, you know."

Mindy Salas was an expat from New York who had married Leo Salas, who was from Costa Rica. They moved down to Costa Rica after a couple years of marriage, having tired of New York City living.

They moved to his hometown of Heredia—a city near San José, the capital of Costa Rica. The Salas wanted to live on the beach, so after a couple years of city living in Heredia, they made the move to Mariposa Beach.

Mindy and Leo had been in the restaurant business for almost their whole lives. In fact, they had met at a New York City restaurant where she was the pastry chef and he was the sous-chef.

They opened their cafe in Mariposa Beach a few years ago, and it had become a roaring success with made-from-scratch bagels and cream cheese, and coffee beans that were sourced from Leo's family's coffee farm.

Dana and Mindy had become friends since Dana moved to the small beach town six months ago, and Mindy had encouraged Dana to open the bookstore.

"The closest bookstore is one hundred fifty miles away in San José, and besides, I'll send business your way, since I don't have a place for customers to sit, which people constantly complain to me about," Mindy had told Dana when she had first asked her about her business idea.

Mindy had reassured Dana that she knew all about the doubt and fears she was having about opening her own business —a scary proposition made even scarier due to the fact that they were foreigners in Costa Rica. It made things more complicated and scarier.

And Mindy had her husband, Leo, who was a Costa Rican —a tico, as Costa Ricans call themselves—who knew the ins and outs of his own country, unlike Dana, who was on her own.

Although she wasn't really on her own. She had good friends like Mindy, and her best friend, Courtney, back in California, who was encouraging her.

Dana also had Benny Campos on her side. Benny was a tico and Dana's attorney, and had helped her navigate the rough waters of moving to Costa Rica and inheriting her uncle's property.

When Dana's cousin contested her uncle's will that left everything to Dana, it was Benny that represented her in court, and when her cousin was murdered within days of her moving to Mariposa Beach and the Costa Rican homicide detective suspected her, it was Benny and her best friend, Courtney— who had flown down to Costa Rica with Dana to help her settle in—that helped her get through that dark period of her life.

"You're at the point of no return, I can tell," Mindy said with a grin.

"You're probably right."

"So what are you waiting for? Call Luis."

"I have to go home first. Benny is coming over to make sure I have all my ducks in a row."

"Stop stalling," Mindy said.

Dana smiled. Mindy could see right through what she was doing.

THREE

Dana made the quick drive back to Casa Verde, the green house. It was nestled in the lush green forest, thus its name. It was a beautiful home with views of the Pacific Ocean, and was located within walking distance to the white-sand beach. She was still incredulous that her estranged uncle had left her such a magnificent property.

Her uncle, Blake Kirkpatrick, had been a travel writer and surfer who came to Costa Rica to surf in the seventies and fell in love with the Nosara area and the country.

He bought the land in the early eighties and built a beautiful home on the land with sweeping views of the Pacific Ocean in front of the property and the lush greenery of the Costa Rican jungle behind it.

Dana continued to battle the feelings that she was a freeloader for inheriting the property and the insecurities of being the newcomer expat to the small tight-knit beach community that was Mariposa Beach.

But every day those feelings kept getting smaller, and her love for the area and the town kept growing.

Dana drove up to a large, green, metal front gate. A tall wall surrounded the property so that people on the other side of it could not peer inside. Dana pressed on a clicker that brought the gate to life as it began to open. She drove in and pressed the button once again, this time to close the gate.

Ramón Villalobos, the caretaker, was working on the yard, swinging his machete like Leonard Bernstein in front of his orchestra.

He stopped and waved as Dana drove by.

Dana looked around but couldn't see Ramón's wife, Carmen.

The Villalobos lived in a small house on the property, and although at first Dana felt the arrangement was odd, she honored her uncle's wishes to allow Ramón and Carmen to continue living there and taking care of the property. She looked back at Ramón, who had gone back to work with his machete, and she smiled. She couldn't imagine what she would do without Ramón and Carmen in her life.

She parked and walked up the front steps leading up to her front door. As soon as she stepped inside, she saw her shorthair white cat coming her way to greet her as if he were a dog.

"Hey, Wally," Dana said to the purring feline as it rubbed up and down her leg, arching its back in excitement.

Dana had always considered herself more of a dog person and never thought about having a cat as a pet, but Wally had been a stray cat who barged in one night and never left.

Dana gave him dishes with water, milk, eggs, ham, and bacon, and she let Wally have the run of the house. *Why would he leave?* she thought as she watched him stretch and yawn. He was sweet and friendly enough, and she quickly became a cat person.

"We'll be hanging out someplace new in a couple months," Dana said to Wally, who just meowed.

"How do you feel about being a bookstore cat during the day?"

"Meow." Wally shook, and fur floated in the air.

"Well, you have no choice but to keep me company in my new bookstore. Besides, a cat and a bookstore go together like peanut butter and jelly."

Her mind was made. She didn't need to wait for Benny. She scratched Wally a few more times, then she walked to the living room, fidgeting with her phone, to call Luis Padilla. He picked up right away.

"Hi, Luis, I'll take it."

The next couple of months she became Bob the Builder in order to spruce up the home of her future bookstore. The video store that used to be there had closed a couple years ago and the property sat empty all that time, so there was a lot of work to be done.

She loved every minute of the process. This is what she needed. She was only in her mid-thirties, way too young to hang around the beach doing nothing productive with her life. She had moved down to Mariposa Beach for the beach living and slower-pace lifestyle, but that didn't mean going into stasis mode at thirty-five.

The bookstore kept her busy and gave her life some pep. Not that it was all ra-ra-ra and fun all the time. There were days where she wanted to say forget it. Never open. Take her losses. Chalk it up as a life lesson and get under the covers and stay in bed for a few months instead.

But she soldiered on. Her friend and lawyer, Benny Campos, had put her in contact with Rodrigo Rosales, whom everyone called Rodri.

Rodri was a contractor who could do it all—carpentry, plumbing, and even working as an electrician. He had done work for just about everyone in town, including Mindy, Benny, and Dana's uncle.

He was a handyman extraordinaire who transformed Dana's vision into a reality after a lot of hard work.

For months there was so much hammering and sawing going on that at night those were the sounds Dana would hear in her sleep. And she would be so tired by the time her head hit the pillow that not even Napoleon, the loudmouth howler monkey that loved to keep her up at night, could pull her out of her dog-tired sleep.

Then there were also constant trips to Nicoya, the county seat and largest small town in the peninsula, which, to Dana's surprise, had a very decent and well-stocked hardware store.

Rodri had explained that there had been a lot of construction going on during the boom days, so the hardware store was accustomed to dealing with contractors and the supplies they needed.

There were a couple times she needed supplies the hardware store in Nicoya didn't have, so she and Benny made the trip to Ferretería EPA—a large hardware store in the capital which was Costa Rica's version of Home Depot.

To her delight, she could order supplies not available at the local hardware store online at EPA's website and they sent a truck down to make the deliveries. She only needed to do that a couple times, but her fears of having to scrounge for supplies had been quickly assuaged. And with Rodri as her foreman, she paid tico prices for the needed supplies, thus avoiding the gringo markup.

"Gringo" was the word used by ticos for English-speaking foreigners. It didn't matter if you were American, European, or Canadian—you were a gringo. And although at first Dana bristled at being referred to as a gringa, she found out that although it could be used for derogatory purposes, it was mostly used without any malicious intent.

Costa Ricans loved giving everyone and everything a nickname, including themselves, thus you weren't a Costa Rican—you were a tico or tica.

FOUR

While Rodri was busy working away at the store, Dana was back home going through the large inventory of books she had there, all thanks to her dead uncle.

Rodri had built Dana's uncle a cozy reading and writing room off of the living room. It was tucked away behind a half door, giving the impression that it was the doorway to a small cellar, but once inside, the truth was revealed that there was a beautiful custom-built library on the other side of that door.

Rodri, who had proudly told Dana that it was his pride and joy of everything he had built in his career, had built it to Uncle Blake's specifications.

She could see why he was proud; it was a real testament to his carpentry skills and his craftsmanship.

It wasn't a big room because of space limitations, but that had been the reason Uncle Blake had chosen it. He wanted a cozy nook where you would lose track of time, not knowing if it was day or night, rainy or sunny. A place to get lost in books or in writing.

The room only measured around six hundred square feet,

but its walls were designed to be bookshelves, so from the floor to the ceiling there were bookshelves made from exotic cocobolo wood.

A hooked ladder flanked the entire length of the shelf from a metal bar on the ceiling. Small wheels on the bottom of the ladder rested in a floor track that extended the entire length of the bookshelves, making it easy to slide the ladder from the right and to the left for easy access to any of the books that were jam-packed onto the shelves.

In the middle of the room was a desk where Uncle Blake and now Dana did their writing.

There was a comfy reading chair next to the desk, but Dana preferred to sit outside in the upstairs veranda so she could listen to the waves crashing yonder and look up to enjoy the views of the Pacific Ocean and the jungle tapestry, instead of feeling like a Keebler Elf in the small room.

It had taken her a while after moving in, but Dana was close to finishing cataloging the thousands of paperbacks that her uncle had stuffed on the shelves over the years.

And even though she felt like she wanted to keep some for herself, she stopped herself. A book on the shelf was just that—a book on a shelf that no one else would be able to enjoy and read, so they would be part of her bookstore's inventory.

Dana sat on the floor with her laptop next to her as she cataloged books in a software program developed by her friend Bucky.

Bucky Moreland was Dana's Silicon Valley friend, who was worth millions of dollars thanks to his programming skills and working for several successful tech start-ups. Eventually Bucky became what many start-up millionaires become, semi-retired and a venture capitalist for fun and money.

He became so excited about Dana's bookstore that he wrote a bookselling software for her.

"Bucky, you didn't have to do that," Dana had told him when he emailed her the program.

"It's no big deal. I used an open-source code I found on GitHub and just spiffed it up for you."

Dana knew that meant he had taken a Ford Pinto and rebuilt it into a Ferrari.

Bucky called it Mariposa Bookz—yes, Bookz with a Z, because Silicon Valley techies loved coming up with alternative spellings for common words.

The software program even had a fancy logo of a book which would open, and a floating blue morpho butterfly, the namesake of the town, would fly out from the book's pages, fluttering its wings as the software loaded.

It was fantastic book-inventory-management software. All Dana had to do was enter the ISBN, International Standard Book Number—the ten- or thirteen-digit number that identifies a specific book—and Bucky's software would do its magic of looking up the ISBN, identify the book, and provide a price-comparison check based on the websites of independent bookstores, eBay, Abebooks, Barnes and Noble, and Amazon.

Not that Dana had to worry about competition. If a customer could save a few bucks ordering online, the shipping cost of getting a book sent to Mariposa Beach would make buying from her bookstore the cheaper and more efficient option, even if it was priced higher.

Dana looked around at the stack of books she wanted to get through for the day. She figured she was about eighty percent done going through and cataloging all of the books. It was a task that would be tedious even for a book lover like Dana if it weren't for the fun she had looking at some intricate book covers and discovering some long-forgotten favorite book that took her back in time to when she had first read it.

Wally the cat curled up on the chair, napping as usual.

Dana found it was best to limit herself to one-hour book-cataloging shifts. After that, she would start to gloss over, wanting to curl up with Wally on the chair for a nap.

She had been at it for about half an hour, going over the same process, book after book. She'd pick up a book from the pile, then she would flip it over to its back cover, locate the ISBN, enter it into the software, hit the enter button, and in mere seconds, Bucky's software did its magic. Once she had all the information, she would click on a "Compile" button and the software would add a price to that particular book, creating a price sticker for the book and also adding it to her inventory database.

Once that was done, she could then print a barcode sticker and its price tag, which she would attach to the book, rendering it ready for sale.

It was a simple process, but tedious. She looked at her inventory, and she was up to 882 books. "Now that's a nice-sized little indie bookstore right there," she said out loud, waking Wally from his nap. He lolled his head from the chair and gave her a quizzical look, then went back to sleep. Dana smiled. She then yawned loudly and stretched and went back at it.

After three one-hour shifts, she was ready to call it a day. "Three hours is more than enough of this," she said, standing up. She groaned as her achy bones protested the three hours spent arched over books and typing into a laptop.

Wally had moved from the comfy chair and was sprawled over a pile of books on the floor, sleeping.

"That doesn't even look comfortable, you crazy cat."

Dana's mobile phone trilled. She looked at her text messages. It was from Benny Campos, and she felt her heart beat a little faster.

He was on his way.

"I guess I can catalog a few more books while I wait for Benny," Dana said to the cat, who did not seem interested.

She smiled as she thought of Benny's text.

FIVE

Benny Campos lived in Escazú, a suburb of the Costa Rican capital city of San José, which was about a four-hour drive from Mariposa Beach.

His family had long owned a beach home located in the outskirts of town in the opposite direction from where Dana lived. But in the small town, it was less than a ten-minute drive from Benny's home to Casa Verde.

Benny had lost his mother in his late teens, and when his father passed away ten years ago, he had inherited the house. He was an only child, so the property was all his.

Dana kept thinking how Benny was spending a lot of time coming down to Mariposa Beach. When she had first met him, he had told her he couldn't make it down as often as he liked because of his law practice in the city and his nine-year-old daughter, but now he seemed to come down every weekend.

And why wouldn't he? It's beautiful and peaceful compared to the hectic and congested city, Dana would tell herself when she fantasized with the idea that perhaps he was spending more and more time at his beach house because *she* was living in town now.

An idea planted in her head by Mindy, who kept reminding Dana that Benny never used to spend as much time down in Mariposa Beach until she came to town.

Benny had arrived late the night before. He preferred to travel during off-peak times to avoid the maddening traffic caravan on Costa Rica's mostly two-lane highway between Mariposa Beach and Escazú, so that meant he usually hit the road at four in the morning or late in the evening.

Ten minutes after his text to let her know he was on his way, she heard the sound of gravel under tires. He had arrived.

She figured that Ramón had opened the front gate for him, since he had been a familiar face around Casa Verde for years, first as her uncle Blake's attorney and now as Dana's lawyer and friend.

Dana had told him via text that he could just walk in and that she was in the library working on the store's inventory, but she knew he didn't like to just walk in unannounced like he owned the place, so she heard his voice coming from the front entrance of the house. "I'm here."

"In the library," she shouted out over her shoulder as she got to her feet. Wally dove from the pile of books he was perched on and scurried away as Benny made his way inside.

"Hey, little guy," he managed to say as Wally bolted towards the living room. Benny watched him beeline to a couch that seemed to be one of Wally's favorite spots to chill.

Dana hadn't seen Benny in a week, and she couldn't believe how fast her heart was beating in anticipation, even though she tried hard to ignore it.

"Hi there," Benny said. He had two large to-go cups of coffee from Mindy's cafe.

"Ooh, you're the best," she said, taking the cup of coffee.

They hugged, and he kissed her on the cheek—not that it

was a romantic gesture, it was the standard way of greeting between friends and even strangers in Costa Rica.

Dana felt lightheaded in his arms, even though it was just for a second or two.

Benny had olive skin, with brown hair and eyes. Like Dana, he was thirty-five years old and divorced. He had a nine-year-old daughter that lived with her mother in San José. Her name was Beatrice. Dana had met her a couple times when she came down to spend the weekend at the beach house. She seemed like a polite, well-mannered little girl.

"Did you bring Beatrice down for the weekend?"

"Not this weekend. She had plans with her friends that trumped hanging out with her old man. A nine-year-old with plans, can you believe that?"

Dana laughed. "Well, she would probably be bored out of her mind here. I've been cataloging one book after the other."

"I can see that. It looks like you made a lot of progress, though," Benny said, looking at a bunch of books in her done pile.

"Getting there."

"Luis Padilla called me. He said you were ready to move forward with the purchase," Benny said, smiling.

"Well, I figured I've spent all this time cataloging these books, so I might as well try and sell them. Besides, it's about time I open the darn bookstore rather than thinking about it all the time."

They shared a laugh. Dana had been hemming and hawing about opening the bookstore for months, and Benny was usually her sounding board. She figured he was probably relieved that the *should I or shouldn't I* talk would be over.

"Congratulations. Luis emailed me the paperwork. I'll take a look at it tonight or tomorrow so you can get ready to open your bookstore," Benny said, sounding excited.

Dana gulped.

"But before that, let me help you get that inventory ready for prime time," Benny said, sitting on the floor next to a pile of books. Dana had been ready to call it a night, but she smiled, happy to accept the help, and she sat back down in front of a pile of books.

They worked side-by-side for about an hour, cataloging more books, when Benny suggested they move the reading chair into the living room so they could have more room for the done pile.

"Great idea."

Benny grabbed the oversized chair.

"You want me to grab the other side?"

"I got it. It's bulky, but it's not that heavy. You can grab the door, though."

Benny carried the chair towards the door, angling its legs first so it could go out the oddly shaped door, and he set it down in the living room. Wally looked up from the couch. He didn't seem too interested in what Benny was up to.

With that out of the way, Dana rolled up the area rug where the chair had been on and she looked down at the floor, puzzled.

Benny walked back into the library and saw Dana staring down at the floor.

"Is that a trap door?" he asked, now joining her in staring at it.

"Looks that way."

The door was flush to the wooden floor, and with the rug over it, you couldn't tell it was under there, which was why Dana hadn't noticed it even though she had been living in Casa Verde for months.

"You didn't know that was there?" Dana asked.

Benny had been her uncle Blake's attorney, and he knew the house better than she had before she moved into it.

"No. Your uncle never mentioned it. This was pretty much his only hands-off part of the house. Aside from Carmen cleaning, I don't think anyone came in here much. Your uncle called it his Fortress of Solitude."

Dana looked at Benny, confused.

"From Superman." Benny blushed at his geekiness.

"Oh, yeah, that place made from ice or whatever," Dana said.

Benny smiled. "Something like that."

"Rodri didn't tell you about this? He must have built it for your uncle."

"No, he didn't tell me about it."

"Well, let's see what's in there," Benny said, sounding excited.

He knelt down and there was a simple latch without a lock, so he unhooked it.

There was a small indentation carved into the trap door that served as its handle. Benny wrapped his fingers in it and pulled it open.

The trap door made a creaking sound like from a horror movie, causing Benny and Dana to look at each other and laugh.

"Creepy," she said.

"Just needs some WD40," Benny responded.

The trap door was on two hinges that propped it open. Benny stepped back so he could look down into the dark, open space below.

There were wooden steps leading down into what looked like a root cellar. Dana and Benny looked at each other, excited about what might be down there.

It was dark, so Benny used the flashlight from his iPhone and shone it down the steps, peering down below.

"Do you see anything?" Dana asked.

"There are several plastic storage bins down there. I think we just found your uncle's storage room."

Dana shone her own iPhone flashlight in there to get a good look.

"It's an underground cellar like we have in California," Dana said.

"You don't see underground cellars and basements like this in Costa Rican homes," Benny said as he began to make his way down the steps. It was a cramped space.

He was six feet tall, so he had to stoop low to make his way down there.

Dana stuck her head through the trap door and could tell there was only room for one person at a time, so she stayed above ground, shining the flashlight down the hole, which was fine with her. The hole was creeping her out.

After a few seconds of Benny being down there, Dana asked, "Any dead bodies down there?"

"No, just bins. Well, unless there is a body in these containers."

Dana could just about see the grin on his face. "Creeping me out, Benny."

He laughed. "I can't tell what's in these bins."

"How about snakes, rodents, or bugs down there? That might be worse than a dead body."

"Clear of snakes, bugs, and rodents," Benny said, turning to look up at Dana from down below. "I'm going to open up one of these boxes."

After about a minute of rustling around down there, he looked up the steps at Dana again and said, "Looks like stuff wrapped up neatly in plastic. I'm bringing one of these containers up."

The container was heavy, but Benny was able to haul it up the steps. Dana grabbed one end of the container and pulled as

Benny pushed from down below, until a blue plastic storage bin had firm footing up above.

Nothing too spooky, Dana thought as she looked it over.

Benny climbed up the stairs and joined Dana back in the library. He gave the container another look. "Just a storage container. Dime a dozen at Office Max," he said.

"Too small for a dead body," Dana said, smiling.

"Unless he placed different body parts in each container," Benny said with a grin.

"I don't even want to think about that!"

Benny removed the lid to the container and they both peered inside. There appeared to be several documents, each one well wrapped in plastic bubble wrap.

Benny pulled out one of the items from the box and carefully removed the shrink-wrap like a plastic surgeon removing a wraparound bandage from a patient's face.

It took a few seconds to remove the layers of plastic and tissue paper, but eventually the contents of the careful wrapping were revealed.

"It's a book," Dana said.

SIX

It took over twenty minutes, but in the end, Benny dragged out several plastic storage boxes from the cellar and brought them back up to the surface.

Dana had to rearrange her book piles to make room for the bins. Next, they carefully removed the lid from each one and examined its contents.

Each box was filled with books and a few comic books; each item was individually wrapped in plastic wrap.

"The level of care with which he stored these books is something. They must be very valuable," Benny said, looking inside one of the bins.

Dana nodded in agreement.

"Let's be very careful with these," Dana said. She began to remove the items from one of the boxes. "I feel like we should be wearing white gloves like they do in the museums and auction houses when handling valuable items," she said nervously as she began to pull out one book after another from the box.

"Uncle Blake never mentioned that he had expensive books down here?"

"No, he never mentioned it, which is odd, since it should

have been part of his estate. If these are really valuable, I should have known," Benny said.

"They must be valuable. Why put in all the time and effort into storing each item like he did and then hide them away in a hidden compartment he didn't tell anyone about?"

Benny nodded in agreement.

The first book she unwrapped was F. Scott Fitzgerald's *Tender is the Night*.

Dana inspected it closely, looking at the front and back cover. It looked old, but it was in excellent condition.

"This looks really old. I don't see an ISBN on it," she said.

"So what does that mean?" Benny asked.

"ISBNs were introduced in 1970, so this must not be a reprint of the novel, since those would have an ISBN assigned to them. I'm thinking that it must be from before 1970."

Dana looked at the front matter. The only publishing date listed there was 1934.

"Could this be a first edition?" Dana asked nervously.

She carefully put the book down and switched over to her laptop and began to tap at it for about a minute. She found what she was looking for. She made an audible gasp, putting her hand over her mouth, embarrassed by the sound she made.

"What is it?" Benny asked, trying to steal a peek at her laptop's screen.

"Benny, if this is really a first edition F. Scott Fitzgerald, it could be worth over ten thousand dollars."

Benny gasped even louder than Dana had.

"For one book?" he asked incredulously in a high-pitched voice.

"Yep. For one book," Dana replied, looking at the plastic storage boxes filled with several individually wrapped books. She wondered what other valuable treasure troves might be hiding inside.

"If these are all filled with first editions, you're looking at a fortune," Benny said.

Dana had been ready to finish cataloging since before Benny arrived, but their find made her too excited to stop, so Benny and Dana spent a couple hours opening the boxes and carefully removing each item from the storage container.

They gently placed the books on the floor because the desk wasn't big enough and they didn't want to stack the books on top of each other.

Once everything was laid out on the floor, they counted over one hundred books and fifty comic books. They spent another hour meticulously and carefully removing each item from its plastic wrapping.

Dana looked up a few more of the titles, surprised by what her quick cursory online research was revealing.

"Oh, my, according to this website, a first-edition copy in good condition of *Casino Royale* by Ian Fleming is worth around thirty thousand dollars," Dana said, holding in her hand a copy in mint condition of that very book.

"Really? A James Bond book?" Benny sounded incredulous. "I can imagine big prices for some fancy literary works like that one from F. Scott Fitzgerald, but a James Bond book is worth that much money? Wow."

A few of the other titles weren't valued as high but still fetched from $1,000 to $5,000 per title.

Dana stepped back after researching around twenty of the books for which she estimated a value of around one hundred thousand dollars, and she still had more than eighty titles she hadn't looked up yet.

"This could be worth in the low end of around one hundred thousand dollars, maybe even two hundred thousand dollars," Dana said, picking up a James M. Cain novel and looking at it gently.

Benny scratched his head and rubbed the back of his neck. He had no idea how expensive first-edition books could be.

"This is crazy. I've heard about baseball cards and comic books being worth a lot of money to collectors, but I had no idea books like these could be worth so much. It's not like you have the Gutenberg Bible or the Declaration of Independence in there."

"I'm not even sure how I can check and verify that these are really first editions," Dana said. But she was pretty sure that they were looking at a very valuable collection of books.

"I don't even know what to do next," she said, sounding frustrated.

Benny was clueless too. "I don't think there are any book experts we can reach out to in Costa Rica," he said.

"We'll have to find someone who is an expert, who can help us."

Benny and Dana also agreed to search the house from top to bottom to see if her uncle had left a notebook or a ledger or a spreadsheet or something that could help them figure out what they had in their hands.

Dana spent the following week scouring every nook and cranny of Casa Verde, moving furniture and rugs, just in case there were more hidden trap doors, but she didn't find any other hidden treasures even though she kept imaging there were more hidden secrets. She even looked at the garden and the acres of property she now owned and wondered what else her eccentric uncle could have hidden out there.

She had asked Rodri about the cellar and he confirmed he had built the hidden cellar as per the specifications of her uncle and was sworn to its secrecy. He also confirmed that he didn't build any other secret rooms in the house.

Rodri wanted to know what she found down there. "Gold, silver, diamond, cash?" he asked excitedly. He had assumed that's why Uncle Blake wanted him to build a storage area underground with strict instructions not to tell anyone about it. Rodri figured he was going to stash valuables down there, so he never told anyone, because if word got out, armed thugs would have invaded Casa Verde.

Rodri was a hardworking, honest man, and he liked Uncle Blake, who treated him well and paid him well, so he made sure not to gossip, since loose lips could pose a great danger to the man.

When Dana told him there were books down there, he seemed utterly disappointed that they had *only* found books.

"I guess it makes sense," Rodri said after Dana told him about the books.

"What makes sense?"

"He was very concerned about dampness and it being too cool in the cellar, so he wanted to make sure I had it well insulated so he could store papers down there. I assumed he meant important documents, not books."

Dana smiled. She didn't bother to explain to him that the value of those books was just as valuable as precious metals, if not more.

She spent days going through the books, and the more she found out about the value of the first editions she now owned, the more she was in shock.

SEVEN

When she had first moved down to Costa Rica, Dana had heard from the expat community that time seemed to slow down to a snail's pace in the tropics, especially in comparison to the hectic pace of life in America.

She had found that there was some truth to such claims, but not in the month that had passed since she and Benny had made the book discovery in her uncle's secret cellar.

It had been quite the opposite—it felt like she had blinked and thirty days had gone by.

And she not only was engrossed in the treasure trove of books she had found, but she had also been busy getting the bookstore ready for prime time.

She spent mornings researching the books from the cellar. She had no doubt that they were all first editions that would have to be independently verified, but it would be a while until she would go to that next stage. Since finding the treasure trove of books, she focused on cataloging and trying to determine the range of each book's value under the assumption they were first editions. All the books were in terrific condition, which she knew increased their value.

Her eyes opened up as to the possible value of the collection when a San Francisco friend with connections to the literary world put her in connection with a friend in the New York City publishing industry, who in turn referred her to an expert in rare books in the city.

His name was Greyson Bay, and he was the man the big auction houses went to when they needed a book appraised.

Dana had been in almost constant contact with Greyson as she tried to determine the value of her newfound book collection.

Greyson owned and operated *Sheep Meadow Rare Books* on Madison Avenue in New York City.

He was a third-generation rare-book dealer who bought and sold books from a fourth-floor office in a ten-story building on Madison Avenue that went back one hundred years.

Dana could tell from their Skype video calls that his office and book room were overstuffed with thousands of books. He also told her he had two off-site storage units with even more collectibles.

He came off a bit snobby, which didn't surprise her, since that was usually par for the course when she had dealt with art dealers as well. His website claimed he had books worth six figures and that not that any Joe, Dick, and Mary off the street could waltz into *Sheep Meadow Rare Books* to peruse his book-shelves—visits were by appointment only and he vetted each inquiry thoroughly. He hated wasting time on book-loving looky-loos who couldn't afford his prices.

Most of the business was done online and via a print catalog he mailed out quarterly to his mailing list of bibliophiles.

When she first called him, he was dismissive and rude. She assumed he figured someone living in some off-the-beaten path beach town in Costa Rica wouldn't have access to the rare books he sought. But since she was given his number by a well-respected publisher, she figured he reluctantly took her call just to tell the publisher he did as he was asked.

She could sense he was eager to blow her off until she began to ask about a first-edition F. Scott Fitzgerald's *Tender is the Night* as well as a first-edition *Fahrenheit 451* by Ray Bradbury.

That seemed to have piqued his interest.

"You have both those books in your possession?" he asked in an incredulous tone.

"I'm looking at them right now," she replied.

Dana had meticulously catalogued what she called the trap door collection, and she agreed to email the spreadsheet she had put together to Greyson late in the evening, Costa Rica time. He had responded in less than three minutes even though it was well past midnight in New York.

They video-chatted the next day, and Greyson Bay went from indifferent and aloof when they had first spoken over the phone to downright friendly and charming right after she showed him a couple of her books over video chat.

He had a round face with small, beady black eyes. He was bald, with just a patch of hair left in front that was so faint that it looked like the three-day stubble he was sporting on his face. The stubble on his face and head were pitch-black, as were his thick eyebrows. His voice was deep and nasally with a thick New York accent that sounded like Barry White if he had been from Brooklyn. He looked clammy and pale, which Dana notched up to him spending a lot of time indoors with his books.

He came off a bit smarmy, but there wasn't any doubt that Greyson Bay was an expert in rare books, and he was the type of person she needed to talk to in order to figure out just what she had discovered in that cellar.

Since the first video chat, they had spent the past week going through Dana's trap door collection, and his unofficial appraisals of her collection staggered her.

Dana was on a video call with Greyson that evening, and he seemed excited.

"I have a buyer for your two Ian Fleming first editions. I really need to get down there or for you to send them to me so I can verify them."

Dana had told Greyson from the start that she wasn't sure what she would do with her collection, but she knew for sure that selling them wasn't in the picture for now. She was busy with her bookstore's grand opening, and living in Mariposa Beach made it more challenging. Even though she had told him this repeatedly, he still pushed her to sell her books.

"Greyson, I've told you I'm not looking for buyers. I'm not sure what I'll do with these books. I'm just trying to find out what I have here, is all. I'm happy to pay you for your consulting time and when and if I'm ready to sell, I'll have you broker that, but for now I'm not interested in selling."

She could see the frustration in his face. "I know, but I just wanted to let you know that I have a collector in London hot to trot. He's offered to buy them sight unseen, even after I told him I haven't physically seen the books to verify them. He didn't care. He's sure they were first editions from what I told him. Of course, you could hold off for an auction. You'll get a lot more money for these books at auction."

"Greyson, one more time, I'm not ready to sell."

"Well then, just make sure you don't put up any of these rare books in that little bookstore of yours," Greyson said, sounding arrogant and condescending.

"I'm not a numbskull, Greyson. Don't worry, I've stored them like you suggested separate from the books that I will be selling. I would appreciate it if you stopped telling buyers about my collection until I'm ready to actually start putting these books up for sale. *If* I decide to sell them."

"All right, all right, Scout's honor," Greyson said, giving Dana the three-finger Boy Scout's salute.

Dana ended the video call and sighed.

She appreciated the help Greyson Bay had been giving her in appraising the book collection and that he had even offered to fly down from New York City to Mariposa Beach to inspect the books personally, since that was the only way he could give an accurate appraisal. But Dana felt like that was moving too fast. She had just discovered this valuable collection of first-edition books a few weeks ago, so she wasn't ready or willing to start selling them with a book broker she had only just met online.

She offered to pay Greyson for his consulting work, but he had refused. So her conscience was clear. Besides, she was too busy with getting her bookstore ready for prime time.

In two short weeks, the doors to Mariposa Books would open—a thought that excited and terrified her. She would deal with the trap door books later. And she told Greyson as much, that she wouldn't be able to talk to him until next month once her bookstore was opened and she had more time to think about her trap door book collection.

EIGHT

It had been a hard slog for the metamorphosis of her retail store in Ark Row to occur.

Dana had the old, rusty, and bent-up metal shelving that once held VHS tapes removed and sent to the scrap metal heap, where she imagined it would end up on a slow boat to China.

In the middle of the store was a large bar-like piece of furniture made from cheap plywood that had long ago seen its better days.

It was to that counter that those customers would bring their videotapes for rental to the employee minding the store.

Dana had it removed and replaced with a much nicer-looking and sturdy counter where she would now mind the store as customers brought books up to the counter for purchase.

She liked to close her eyes and visualize it, and it always made her smile.

The store's flooring was a mess. She didn't know if the floor had been covered with carpet at one time or another, but she was left to work with what looked like a badly stained garage slab. To make matters worse, the natural porosity and chalkiness of concrete made it difficult to really clean. It didn't make sense to install carpet in the subtropical climate weather of the Guanacaste Province, so she went with an epoxy coating, transforming the floor from stained and ugly to a pretty gray color with sprinkled-on flakes that gave it a whimsical, glittery look that was slip-resistant to boot.

The transformation of the store drew a crowd just about every day, which amused Dana. There wasn't much excitement going on in Mariposa Beach, so the locals liked to gather around to actually watch paint dry.

At least one member of the Gossip Brigade seemed to stop by to check on the progress. The brigade was made up of a group of four lifelong friends—although for as much as they argued, it didn't seem possible—who were septuagenarians and octogenarians, and Dana was certain they were letting everyone in town know about the progress of the bookstore.

Let them gossip. Dana was thrilled with the progress. The interior and exterior had been painted, and the shop looked like a million bucks in comparison to how it looked before Dana got to work.

Big Mike, who owned Big Mike's Surf Shop next door, couldn't remember the last time the old video store had a fresh paint job.

"Oh, gnarly, you're painting the video store," he had said when he saw Dana, Benny, and Rodri arrive with his two-man painting crew. "Place needed a fresh coat of paint like ten years ago, bro." Big Mike spoke with the heavy Southern California surfer dude accent that Dana found amusing, since he was originally from Kansas, but he had been a professional surfer who had participated in the invite-only Mavericks big-wave surfing competition in Northern California, so she figured he earned the right to speak like a SoCal surfer versus a Kansas Jayhawk.

Dana went with a bright white color because she wanted

her bookstore to be bright and inviting. The video store had been painted in much darker drab colors.

She figured they went with the darker look because they were probably showing videos, like most of the old video stores had done in the past. All that was left of those days was a large television mount that had been up on the wall, the TV long gone. Dana had that removed, then had the wall patched up and painted white by Rodri, who had enlisted two nephews to help him with the big paint job. Dana was delighted with their work, and the team of three began to make progress even faster.

Next up was the shelving. She didn't want the look of a stuffy, traditional bookstore with shelves overflowing with books. She wanted the look of a newsstand. Perhaps subconsciously it had been a nod to her days as a newspaper reporter, but she just liked the look of newsstand shelves where the magazines were stacked facing out so visitors could see right away what they were looking at. It was a bit trickier to accomplish that look for a bookstore, but she wasn't building a Barnes and Nobles–like behemoth of a bookstore from yesteryear. Mariposa Books was going to be a small bookstore, so she wanted it to have that quaint, cozy feel to it just like the small beach community of Mariposa Beach itself.

Dana was delighted with Rodri's carpentry work, but to her shock, Benny was a skilled woodworker of cabinetry and furniture.

"Woodworking is a hobby," he had told Dana with a shrug. "I have a nice wood shop at my house in Escazú."

"Color me impressed," Dana said.

The end result was light-colored bookshelves made out of birch wood, designed so that books would be shelved with their cover facing out, not the book's spine.

There would also be a section for snacks and coffee, with the goodies provided by Mindy's Cafe across the street.

Dana was shelving books when there was a knock on the door. Luis Padilla, the real estate agent that had found the retail space, wanted a tour.

He whistled his approval of what he saw when Dana showed him around.

"Wow, you've really transformed the old video store. This is amazing."

"Thanks," Dana said, smiling. She stood back to take in all the hard work of the past couple months that it took to get to that point.

After a few minutes, the tour was interrupted by the rattling of the front door that Dana had locked. She was heading towards the door when the person began to knock aggressively.

Dana turned to look at Luis, who rolled his eyes and hissed, "How rude."

Dana unlocked the door and opened it ajar. There was a man standing there whom she hadn't met before.

"Oh, good, you're open," he said, peering into the bookstore. He was an American.

"Actually, we're not; that's why the door was locked. The grand opening won't be for another two weeks, sorry." Dana began to close the door when the man slipped his foot into the door, preventing her from closing it.

Dana looked down at the foot, then she glared at the rude man.

"Well, I'm only here for a week," he said, looking over her head into the store.

"I'm sorry, sir, I'm just not open for business yet."

"I see you have a bunch of books in there. Come on, let me take a look," the man whined.

"Any problems, Dana?" Luis said as he stood behind Dana.

The man removed his foot. "You're not going to stay in business too long by turning away eager customers," the man said angrily.

"Like I've told you more than once, I'm not open for business yet. Sorry," Dana said, closing the door.

"Nice way to treat your customers," the man yelled from behind the closed door.

"Weirdo," Luis said as he walked over to the window and pushed the shade aside so he could look outside to see what the man was doing. "He's leaving," Luis said.

"Good. The nerve of that man," Dana replied. She felt creeped out over the odd encounter.

"I didn't know the bookselling business generated such passion. Perhaps you'll have campers out lining outside like at an Apple store grand opening," Luis said, laughing out loud.

"I wish," Dana said.

She proceeded with her tour of the store, trying to act unfazed in front of Luis, but the encounter with the pushy man left her rattled, so she was not in the mood of being alone in the store, thus she left with Luis Padilla.

"Can't wait for the opening, darling," he said with a wave as he got into his Toyota RAV4 and drove off. Dana fired up Big Red and headed home to Casa Verde, which was a five-minute drive away.

That evening, Dana met up with Benny at the Qué Vista Restaurant, which specialized in local tico cuisine of casados, pescado entero, ceviche, picadillo de papa, arroz con pollo, gallo pinto, and the like. The restaurant was right on the beach, its structure built to resemble a palapa.

The ocean view was so incredible that Dana was certain she

could feel the sea splash reach her table with every crashing wave mere feet away.

She ordered the arroz con mariscos—a seafood stir-fried rice dish that consisted of shrimp, mussels, fish, peas, carrots, onions, and red peppers among other goodies.

Benny ordered the pescado entero—Spanish for whole fish. And it really was the whole fish from head to tail served on a plate with a salad, fried yuca, and lots of fresh lime slices.

If the new bookstore wasn't enough to keep the Mariposa Beach rumor mill fat and happy, the sight of Dana and Benny out for another late-night dinner was going to give it heart palpitations.

They both knew it, and although at first it felt awkward, they stopped caring. "You can't stop a small beach community from gossiping, so I don't worry about it," Benny had explained to Dana when she had brought it up during their last dinner together.

Dana had been relieved he felt the same way as she did on the subject matter. She enjoyed his company, and he was her lawyer who had helped her fend off a lawsuit over the ownership of Casa Verde, and they had become friends.

Besides, for an American expat to open a small business in Costa Rica required a lot of paperwork and legal minefields to cross, and she would have long ago set one of them off without Benny's legal expertise.

She pushed the thoughts of going beyond the friendship zone—something that continued becoming harder for her, especially on a lovely dinner night out like the one they were on, so her mind would wander until she would chide herself... *Stop it, Dana, you're doing it again.*

She needed something to talk about before it got awkward again.

"So, I had my first sort of customer today at the bookstore," she said, eager to get her mind on another subject, even if that subject was the rude tourist.

Benny responded with a quizzical look as he took a sip from his bottle of Cerveza Imperial.

Dana told Benny all about the obnoxious, door-blocking tourist from earlier in the day.

"Maybe they'll start camping out for the grand opening like an Apple store when a new iPhone is about to drop," Benny said, grinning.

"That's exactly what Luis Padilla said."

At that moment there was a loud commotion coming from one of the tables towards the back of the restaurant, by the bar.

"I'm not drunk," shrieked the voice of a man who had obviously imbibed vast quantities of alcohol.

"Looks like someone isn't happy about being cut off," Benny said, looking over towards the bar. Dana turned around for a glimpse and she quickly turned back to face Benny.

"Oh, my, that's him."

"Who?"

"Him. My first wannabe customer today."

"Oh, *him*," Benny said, trying to catch a better glimpse of the man.

He was in his mid- to late thirties and although balding you could tell he was a redhead.

"Seems like a great guy," Benny said facetiously as the man kept raising his voice to protest being cut off.

After a few minutes, the drunken man was making his way out when he locked eyes with Dana and stopped at her table.

"You're that woman from the bookstore," the man said, slurring his words.

Oh, gosh, Dana thought as she looked away, embarrassed.

"Sir, please leave," Benny said, throwing his napkin on the table.

"You wouldn't let me inside your bookstore. I just wanted to look at your books," the man said, sounding more agitated.

"Like I told you this morning, I'm not open for business yet."

"Whatever," the man said, spraying Dana with spittle.

"Oh, gross." She flinched.

"Okay, buddy, that's enough," Benny said, getting up.

"Tell your boyfriend to take it easy, I'm leaving," the man said as he continued on his way outside.

Benny watched the man stagger off as Jorge, the restaurant manager, apologized. María Rivera, the owner, soon joined Jorge to offer her apology, and told them dessert was on the house.

Benny and Dana insisted that wasn't necessary, but she pressed, so two big slices of the deliciously decadent tres leches cake topped with fresh strawberries arrived soon after.

"Enjoy," María said with a smile and wink.

"Well, that's a lot of excitement for Mariposa Beach," Dana said, smiling as she picked up a fork and tore into her dessert.

NINE

The next day, Dana was back at work at the bookstore. She was outside with Rodri and his teenage nephew, putting in some final touch-ups to the exterior. Dana was working on the trim when she heard a rattle coming down Main Street.

It was a rattle she recognized right away, and it made her tense up because she knew what that rattling was: it was the telltale sound of Barry Shy's rickety trike bike, overloaded with junk and trinkets clanging together and against the metal frame of his three-wheeled trike as he headed into town on one of his supply runs. Unfortunately for her, the small grocery store he frequented was on the tail of the Ark Row shops, so he had to pedal down Main Street and by her bookstore, which meant he would see her there. She sighed. The last thing she needed on that pleasant morning was another confrontation with Barry Shy, especially after dealing with the loudmouth tourist at her store and the restaurant the previous day.

Am I wearing jerk-attraction spray? she thought as she put all her attention to the work at hand, trying hard to ignore Barry Shy and his clanking trike as he rode through town.

Barry Shy was anything but shy. He was a sixty-two-year-old American expat who lived in a handmade shack-like cabin a few miles from Mariposa Beach up in the mountains.

He would come into town riding on an old but sturdy-looking Worksman Mover Industrial Tricycle with a large rear-mounted cargo basket. Everyone in town called it his trike.

Dana had thought it was an amazing feat to get around on that thing in the mostly unpaved and pockmarked roads around town, and how he got that overloaded trike back up the mountain dumbfounded her.

She figured the scrawny old man must have the legs of a Tour de France cyclist.

Barry Shy was a self-described minimalist infused with a self-righteous indignation over the commercialization of the world and in particular, and much to his fury, Mariposa Beach.

He would come to town to pick up the few amenities he needed that didn't come from his land, like propane and kerosene, and pontificate on the demise of Mariposa Beach because of the continuous influx of tourists and well-heeled expats.

Dana was the latest expat in town, much to his ire. She had noticed that it seemed to be a popular sport for expats who had arrived long ago to complain about the newest expats in town.

Benny had explained that it was a common phenomenon he saw a lot all over the country, where each new wave of expats would be reviled by the previous wave.

It seemed to her that Barry loathed all expats, and that probably included himself. He seemed like a miserable man, and Dana actually felt bad for the man who lived all alone like a hermit up in the mountain.

Dana had noticed throughout her life that it was hard for people like Barry Shy to like other people when they don't even like themselves.

But his disdain for one type of person trumped them all: the merchants. Barry would chastise the merchants for catering to tourists' every spoiled whim, and Dana's bookstore was the latest affront to his sensibilities since Mindy had opened her coffee and bagel shop a few years ago to sell "fancy and over-priced coffee and bagels to the 'bugs,'" which is what Barry called the tourists.

Tourists were bugs. Expats like Dana and Mindy—and any expat that came to town after him—had their own descriptor. They were locusts.

"He called me a locust. He said I was destroying Mariposa Beach, eating up all the natural resources, and that I was now his enemy for opening a new business in town," a befuddled Dana had told Mindy a few weeks ago, after her first face-to-face confrontation with Barry Shy.

Dana had pushed back and tried to act tough, like he wasn't scaring her, but he had—a fact she would only share with Mindy.

"That man sounds like a broken record. He has said that to all of us at one time or another, so don't worry about it, honey, we're all locusts to him. And tourists are bugs," Mindy explained.

"Hello, he's an expat."

"Yes, but in that indignant, judgmental little brain of his, any expat that moved here after he did and doesn't live out in the jungle in a medieval cabin without electricity or running water like the Unabomber is a locust, since we're consuming all the natural resources and I guess he is not, in his mind."

"What a jerk," Dana said.

"Yes, indeed. But don't worry, honey, being Barry's enemy won't take much of your time. It's just an annoyance. Like a gnat. His self-righteous indignation will eventually zero in on someone new."

"How long has he been here?"

"He's been here a while. I was told that he showed up in the late eighties. I don't know from which state, since he won't tell anyone. He bought land a few miles out of town when it was a lot cheaper back then. When all the hoopla about Y2K ushering in the end of the world, he moved down permanently in the early nineties. I heard when he first came to town, he had a tent and a few sacks of rice and beans as he prepared for the end of the world. Well, Y2K came and went and nothing happened, but he stayed on and has never left. He eventually built that shack he lives in now."

"Is it nice?"

"Oh, no, not at all," Mindy replied, laughing. "It's slanted to one side, since he's not a very good carpenter. But he does have a nice little farm going now. His cabin has no electricity, no water, or indoor bathroom. He doesn't have a phone or a computer. I would be surprised if he even knew what Facebook or Twitter were, seeing how he's been out there alone and disconnected since the nineties."

"That's so sad." Dana actually felt bad for the man. It was obvious there was some sort of mental issue going on there.

"I think he gets lonely out there, so when he comes to town, he picks fights with one of us locusts as a way to connect with fellow human beings, then he scampers back to his shack."

It sounded like an awful way to live to Dana, but to each their own. She just wished he respected her choice to be part of the community and to start a business, just like she respected his choice of living like a hermit disconnected from the world.

Dana was trying to ignore him. She glanced at the window

to catch his reflection, hoping he would continue to pedal into town without stopping to give her grief.

She was relieved that he kept on pedaling by her store without saying anything. After yesterday's encounters with the loudmouth, she wasn't in the mood for more drama.

TEN

Dana was stocking her bookshelves when Ramón showed up around noon in his 1997 Datsun pickup with several boxes of books from Casa Verde. Dana was excited to finish stocking up her bookstore.

He moved the boxes from the bed of his pickup truck into the store.

"Do you need my help putting these away?" he asked, always eager to lend a helping hand.

"No, it's fine. Benny is coming. And I have Rodri and his nephew Mateo here. So I have plenty of help."

Ramón smiled and left. Dana figured he was more than happy to go to tend to his landscaping of Casa Verde that he loved.

Benny arrived an hour later to help out putting the books in their appropriate spots.

They were getting a lot done, and Dana was getting into the music of Marimba Orquesta Maribel that Rodri was playing on his iPhone. It was a mixture of salsa, cumbia, reggae, and typical Costa Rican music where the marimba was front and center.

They were all grooving to the beats when they heard muffled shouts coming from outside.

"Oh, brother," Dana said as they made their way outside, where Barry Shy was holding up a sign that read: "Stop the Gentrification of our beaches."

"Oh, brother," Dana said again. She went back inside and closed the door and locked it.

"Don't worry, he does that to every new business until he eventually gets bored and wanders on back to his mountain patch," Benny said, a stack of books under his arm.

"He's such a pain," Dana said.

"That he is. He's been around forever."

"Yeah, Mindy gave me the four-one-one on him when he first showed up to harass me. She said no one knows where he's from originally. Do you know?"

"I don't know either. I don't think anyone knows, and he's not telling. I think he likes the mystery of it all. When people have asked him where he's from, he just says 'Earth.' Rumor has it he's an old hippy from the States who moved to Canada to avoid the Vietnam War draft, but only he knows the truth, and he's not sharing."

"So what's his problem?" Dana wondered.

"Acid flashbacks," Benny said, grinning.

Dana gave him a shrug.

"He's just been here a long time. Lives off the grid. He doesn't make it into town that often anyway, so he's not going to be a problem for you for too long. Eventually he gets bored and moves on. He just likes making some noise and getting attention. Maybe it reminds him of protesting in the sixties or something," Benny explained.

Dana peered out a small gap in the window covering and saw him out there leading his one-man protest of her store.

"I thought he would go easy on you, since you're opening a bookstore. The man loves to read," Benny said.

"Yeah, the Unabomber manifesto, no doubt," Dana said.

Benny laughed. "Don't worry, he will move on."

"I'm used to dealing with self-righteous old hippies. I am from San Francisco, after all. But he just seems like an angry old man that could be dangerous."

"Nah, he's harmless," Benny said.

"I can't have him out there pestering potential customers when the store opens."

"Don't worry, the man has the attention span of a child. He'll wander off before then."

Dana hoped Benny was correct. The grand opening was days away, and she didn't want Barry Shy to ruin her big day.

Dana and Benny continued to work for another hour, stocking books while Rodri and Mateo finished up their work inside. Dana asked Rodri to turn the music up loud to drown out Barry's chants from outside, but she could still hear him ranting and raving.

Once all the books were in place, Dana decided to call it a day.

"I've had enough for today," she told Benny.

She sent Rodri and Mateo home as well.

On their way out, Barry became agitated when he saw them exiting the bookstore, and he seemed to focus all his rage on Dana, the newest expat and town merchant.

"Why don't you go back to the empire?" Barry shouted at her. Dana assumed he meant the States.

"Why don't you go back to the empire, Barry? Don't forget, you're an expat too. A guest in our country," Benny, who was born and raised in Costa Rica, said to him, smiling.

Rodri spoke enough English to understand, and he laughed, being a native Costa Rican as well. The other tico in the group,

Mateo, didn't speak English. But Dana could tell he was aware of the tension, so he stood next to his uncle in case things got physical.

"You sold out to corporate interests, man, you're part of the problem too," Barry spewed his spiel. He refocused on Dana and pointed an arthritic finger at her, seething. "You are turning Main Street into Rodeo Drive. You all are."

Dana looked around and laughed. "I don't know how long you've been down here, but you don't have to worry, my small used-book store won't turn Ark Row into Rodeo Drive, so why don't you chill out and leave me alone?"

"It's not worth to argue with crazy, let's go," Benny said.

They left Barry there shouting his slogans alone as he waved his sign in the air.

On the drive back to Casa Verde, Dana couldn't help but feel shaken by Barry Shy.

She'd had a rough start moving to Mariposa Beach.

Her own cousin contested the last will and testament of her uncle, who had bequeathed Casa Verde to her.

He sued her in California and then in Costa Rica. She had to deal with sleazy real estate agents and real estate developers who wanted to cash in on selling Casa Verde to Gustavo Barca, who Dana viewed as Mariposa Beach's very own Mr. Potter and Mr. Burns rolled into one.

Then her cousin was murdered and the police had her as the prime suspect. It had been a stressful start to living in a tropical paradise.

The trauma of all that began to fade and she decided to start her very first business ever, and now she had a half-baked old coot protesting against her opening the bookstore. She really hoped that Benny was right and that Barry Shy would lose interest and go away back to being a hermit. She just hoped it was sooner rather than later.

She joked about the Unabomber manifesto, but the man even looked like the Unabomber, with his long, unkempt gray hair and beard.

Benny stayed for a beer then he went home. Dana went upstairs to her favorite spot in the house, a wraparound veranda that overlooked her property and the Pacific Ocean. It was too dark to see any of that, but she could hear the sounds of the jungle and the ocean competing for her attention.

She plopped down on her comfy chair out on the veranda with a cup of green tea and a crime novel by William Kent Krueger. She was looking forward to reading more about Cork O'Connor fighting crime in Northern Minnesota.

Wally soon joined her, jumping up to share the chair and shoving his little white furry head against her book. "Stop it, I'm reading," Dana protested. But he didn't care. He wanted attention, so he got it.

"You're spoiled," Dana said, putting down her book and petting her pushy cat as he began to purr wildly.

ELEVEN

The next morning, Dana was at Mindy's coffee house when it opened.

"You're up early," Mindy said as she carried a tray of freshly made jalapeño bagels from the kitchen.

"Working on the bookstore, but I need some coffee and one of your delicious everything bagels with mango cream cheese."

"Coming right up."

Everything at Mindy's coffee house was homemade; bagels, cream cheese, her famous pineapple empanadas, even the coffee beans she used to make her delicious coffee came from Mindy's husband's family farm in Tarrazú.

"I was actually going to call you yesterday, but things got hectic here," Mindy said as she prepared her order. "There was an obnoxious man here yesterday asking a lot of questions about your bookstore. Gave me the creeps."

"What did he look like?"

Mindy described a man who seemed to fit the description of the obnoxious man that tried to barge his way into her bookstore and had made the scene later that night at the restaurant.

Dana told him about her two encounters with that person.

"I wonder if it's the same creep?" Mindy asked.

"What are the odds that two creepy men are so interested in my bookstore?" Dana said, taking the bag with her bagel and a cup of coffee to go.

"Be careful. It's like he's stalking you or something."

"Great. A stalker and Barry Shy in my face."

"Sorry, I heard about Barry protesting outside your store yesterday," Mindy said.

"The man is like a pimple on your rear end. Harmless, but hard to ignore when you try to sit down," Dana said, sighing.

"Barry Shy has been a thorn on the entire community for years. He thinks we should all eschew modern technology and live off the land," Mindy explained.

"So he's all Amish without the charm," Dana said.

Dana and Mindy laughed.

"Well, go on, skedaddle, you have a grand opening in two days!"

Dana went back to work, but she hadn't made much progress before she was interrupted.

"Are you open now?"

Dana turned around and saw the loudmouth standing there with a hangdog expression on his face. *Dang it*, Dana thought. She'd forgotten to lock the door, and he just walked right in.

Rodri and his nephews weren't expected for another hour, meaning she was alone with a man who appeared to be stalking her, which made her very nervous. She looked around and saw the box cutter she had been using, and she picked it up and held it in her hand. She was behind the counter, so he couldn't see it.

"Does it look like we're open?" She couldn't help being snarky to him, but then realized once again she was all alone and he was bigger and heavier than she was. She held onto the box cutter tighter and added, "Sorry, look, we open in two days, please come back then."

"I would like to extend my apologies for the other day and that night at the restaurant. I had a few too many Cuba Libres that night and didn't realize it until it was too late."

"It happens, but I'm afraid I'm still not open. As you can see, I'm still putting the final touches. Come back in two days for the grand opening," Dana said.

"But we're both right here now. How hard is it to just let me peruse your books?"

What is wrong with this guy? Dana thought.

"It doesn't work that way. Sorry."

"I don't understand why you're being so difficult."

"Ditto, Mister," Dana said.

"My name is Chris Smith. I'm from Chicago."

"Well, Mr. Smith from Chicago, come back for the grand opening if you want to look at my books."

"Okay, here is the deal. I'm a book collector. The reason I'm so insistent is because I would like to get a crack at seeing what you have for sale before it's available to the general public. That way I can be sure to pick up a gem or two."

"Believe me, I don't have any collectible gems here, just regular old used books like you would find at any used bookstore in Chicago."

"I'll be the judge of that," Smith snapped.

"Now you're making me feel uncomfortable," Dana said, the box cutter still in her hand.

"Look, I'll pay you a hundred dollars just to look around. Even if I don't find anything I like, you can keep the money."

"Not interested. I'm asking you again to please leave."

Chris Smith didn't make an effort to leave. He just stood

there glaring at her, making Dana even more nervous as she squeezed the box cutter tight in her right hand.

"Hey, Dana, everything okay with this dude?" Big Mike said, stepping inside.

Dana felt a wave of relief at seeing Big Mike standing there dressing down Smith.

"It's cool, Big Mike, Mr. Smith from Chicago was just leaving. Isn't that right?" Dana said, crossing her arms over her chest, the box cutter visible to everyone now.

Chris Smith let out an exasperated breath.

"I swear I'm in the Twilight Zone. This whole town is a joke. Fine. You just lost a good customer."

Smith turned and glared at Big Mike. "You too," he said, and stormed off.

Dana and Big Mike watched him head down Main Street and into the pathway heading up to the luxurious Tranquil Bay Resort.

"He must be doing pretty well for himself if he's staying up at the resort," Big Mike said.

"Thank you, Big Mike," Dana said, giving him a hug.

"No problem. I've seen that dude hanging around your shop. When I saw him come in and figured you were alone, I thought I would check in."

Dana thanked him again. "He's really persistent. Thinks I have valuable books here or something..." Dana said, trailing off into her thoughts. *Hmm. There is no way he could know about the first editions.* Only she, Benny, and Greyson Bay knew about those.

"Earth to Dana." Dana snapped out of her thoughts and looked back at Big Mike, who was smiling. "Deep thought, huh?"

"Yeah, sorry. That guy just has me a little freaked out. Him and Barry Shy and his one-man protest."

"Oh, don't worry about Barry. He's harmless and moves on to annoy other people quickly."

That was what everyone said to her: "Don't worry, he's harmless." It made her think of how friends and neighbors of killers usually said the same thing when describing their harmless friend, family member, or coworker who snapped and went on a killing spree.

Never in a million years did I think he could do something like that. He was so harmless.

Dana shook those thoughts from her head and chatted with Big Mike about the store's progress, giving him a quick tour of the latest updates to the store. He was impressed with the handiwork and progress being made. After about five minutes he left and went back to his surf shop next door.

A few minutes later, Rodri arrived with one of his nephews, Mateo, and she felt much better about getting back to work and not being all alone, just in case Chris Smith or Barry Shy came around again.

She put another full day and finally Rodri was finished with his work. The place had been transformed into a beautiful, sleek, modern-looking, trendy bookstore just like she had imagined. But there were still a lot of things she needed to check off her to-do list before the grand opening, so as she drove home that night, she decided she would wake even earlier than usual tomorrow to get an early running start to her day.

She loaded the last few boxes of books into Big Read before going to bed. She was going to take a nice, long bath and read that novel that Wally wouldn't let her read the previous night. She would have a relaxing glass of red wine then some chamomile and lavender tea, which was her favorite bedtime tea. She would get a good night's rest, then she would be up and running at five in the morning so she could be at her bookstore by five thirty. Since Mindy's Cafe didn't open until seven a.m., she would have to brew coffee at home to bring along.

She crawled into bed. Wally was already there waiting for her. She set her alarm and warned Wally he would not be happy when the band Luscious Jackson would wake them up so early. She was going to have a very productive day, she thought as she drifted off to sleep.

TWELVE

Dana sat on the cherry-red hood of Big Red, her feet resting on the Jeep's front grill. She was in a daze when she heard a car driving fast and then hitting the brakes hard, parking next to Big Red.

She snapped out of her stupor and turned to see Benny's white Toyota Land Cruiser.

The Land Cruiser shook in a rocking motion as Barry threw it into park before coming to a full stop. He jumped out of the SUV with a look of terror on him.

"Are you okay?" he said, sounding concerned.

"I'm fine. But... there's a body inside."

Benny looked towards the bookstore's open door.

"In your bookstore?"

Dana nodded, saying nothing.

Benny turned to go inside.

"Don't go in there, Benny, it's awful. I already called the police, but it will be a while before they get here."

Mariposa Beach was too small of a town—it was more of a village than an actual town—to have its own police force, as was the case with most of the tiny beach communities that dotted the Pacific Coast of the Guanacaste Province of Costa Rica.

Unlike the United States, where just about every town—including small towns—had its own police department or was policed by a nearby county sheriff's department, Costa Rica's law enforcement was set up completely different.

The country had a National Police Force known as the Fuerza Pública de Costa Rica—Public Force of Costa Rica—that had stations and substations across the country.

The closest National Police Station to Mariposa Beach was in Nicoya, a city that served as the main transportation hub to Guanacaste's beaches and national parks, which was about an hour away.

The Fuerza Pública also had small substations, the closest one of those was the Tourism Police unit in Playa Guiones, which was about twenty minutes from Mariposa Beach.

The men and women of the Tourism Police were part of a special unit of the National Police force that focused on keeping tourists and the tourism industry in the region secure. The officers patrolled the beach towns along the coast, including Mariposa Beach, on motocross motorcycles. They were armed and went through the same National police academy as the other cops of the National Police, but since their focus on protecting tourists, other cops teasingly referred to them as *Baywatch Cops*.

"I just want to check it out. Make sure that person really is dead or if we can help him," Benny said, walking towards the bookstore.

"Trust me, he's as dead as disco," Dana said. Her words sent a shiver down her spine.

Benny went inside anyway. He stumbled outside a minute later; it looked like the olive complexion to his skin had been turned to an ashen pallor. He tried to speak, but he was having a difficult time.

"I told you. He's dead."

Benny nodded in agreement as he leaned on Big Red, wishing he hadn't gone inside.

"Freddy will be here soon," Dana said, referring to Freddy Sanchez, a police officer with the Tourist Police unit working out of the Guiones Beach substation. It seemed he was usually the one patrolling Mariposa Beach, although he rarely made it to town unless called to deal with something—a tourist's rental car was broken into, someone was pickpocketed, a beach party getting too loud and too wild, a shoving match at the Giggling Dorado bar, and other usually petty crimes.

Dana just stared at her bookstore that was supposed to open in less than two days, and where there was now a dead body inside.

"Were you able to get a look at who's in there?"

Benny nodded. "You couldn't tell?"

"I saw feet sticking out from the counter and I hightailed it out of there."

"Smart," Benny said, sounding wistful.

"Well? Did you recognize the person?"

Benny nodded slowly.

"Who was it, Benny?"

Benny sighed and looked at Dana with sad eyes.

"It's Barry Shy. He's dead."

"What? Barry? Are you sure?"

Benny nodded again.

"Could you tell what happened to him?"

"I didn't look that close."

They sat in silence for a couple minutes.

"Well, this is not the way I wanted people in the peninsula to hear about my bookstore," Dana said. She felt guilty about thinking and saying that out loud, but it was how she felt at that moment.

Barry Shy was lying dead inside, but she was only human and couldn't help thinking about the impact that would have on the grand opening of her bookstore. Selfish, but she had to think about that.

The next hour was a blur. Freddy Sanchez arrived in his motocross bike about twenty minutes after Benny arrived.

He went inside with his pistol drawn. He came out a few minutes later speaking into his shoulder radio, with his sidearm holstered.

He removed some yellow tape from the side pouch of his motorcycle and he put it up across Dana's front door.

Dana's heart sank as she watched him secure the crime scene. Her bookstore.

"Can you tell how he died?" Dana asked.

"Looks like he was shot, but it will be up to the crime scene people to determine that," Sanchez said as he continued putting up tape.

Dana put her hand to her mouth as Benny tried to comfort her.

She watched Freddy tape up her bookstore and couldn't help but think that in the next couple hours, the other merchants would be arriving to open their stores, only to be confronted with crime scene tape and a bevy of police activity as investigators worked the crime scene which was Dana's bookstore.

"I'm going to check the back, please do not go near the taped-off area," Officer Freddy warned as he held the big roll of yellow tape and wandered around the corner towards the back of the building.

Dana tried to hold back the tears. She heard someone calling her name. It was Mindy, who was crossing Main Street, running towards her.

"What's going on? I got to my coffee shop and saw Freddy's motorcycle and the tape. Are you okay?" Mindy asked.

Dana hopped off the hood of Big Red, realizing she had been sitting there like a hood ornament for almost an hour.

"I'm fine," she said as she hugged Mindy. "It's Barry Shy. He's dead. Inside my bookstore."

"What?" was all Mindy could muster.

"I found the body." Dana began to sob.

"Oh, honey," Mindy said, hugging her tightly. She looked at Benny, who seemed lost, not knowing what to do or say.

A minute later, Officer Freddy returned. He nodded at Mindy and checked to make sure the crime scene was intact.

"Did you find anything back there?" Benny asked.

"Mr. Shy's three-wheel bicycle contraption is back there. Seems he got in from the back."

"How did he get in?" Dana asked.

"He broke in."

Benny, Mindy, and Dana exchanged puzzled looks.

"Barry was a lot of things—a pain in the rear, opinionated, rude, loud—but he wasn't a thief," Mindy said.

"I can't imagine he would burglarize anyone," Benny added.

"Maybe he broke in to sabotage my store so it wouldn't open," Dana said.

"So who shot him, then?" Mindy asked.

"These are all scenarios that will be addressed by the actual detectives when they arrive from Nicoya in about an hour, so I wouldn't put too much effort into these theories. It's best to leave that to the actual professionals who will be tasked with figuring out what happened here tonight," Officer Freddy said.

It was a strange concept for Dana that it would take so long for homicide detectives to arrive, but that's how it was for the small beach communities in the coast

In Costa Rica, only agents from the elite Judicial Investigative Police—known by its Spanish initials for Organismo de Investigación Judicial, OIJ—could investigate crimes.

An OIJ agent was the equivalent of an FBI Special Agent and a city police detective all rolled into one.

They were the crème de la crème of the country's law enforcement system, highly professional and trained. Most OIJ investigators trained at the FBI National Academy, which was an elite program for active US and international law enforcement personnel to enhance their credentials in their field and to raise law enforcement standards and knowledge.

The National Police officers, like Freddy Sanchez, could not investigate crimes, nor could they charge a citizen with a crime. Their duty was to enforce the law and secure the scene, then wait for the OIJ to send down agents to do the actual investigating and assessing of who should be charged with a crime.

"Do you know which OIJ detectives are coming, Freddy?" Benny asked.

"Picado," he replied sheepishly, knowing that wouldn't ease Dana's nerves over the situation of finding Barry Shy dead in her bookstore.

Both Dana and Benny sighed equally loudly.

Unfortunately for Dana, this wasn't the first time she had to deal with OIJ Homicide Detective Juan Mora Picado since moving to Mariposa Beach from San Francisco. When her cousin, with whom she was involved in a legal battle over Casa Verde, had been murdered, Picado was sent down to investigate, and he had zeroed in on her as his prime suspect.

His surly personality made matters worse, and the two of them got along as well as Seinfeld and Newman.

After that case had been resolved and the real murderer was found out, Dana thought she would never have to see Picado again, yet just a few months later, the ornery detective was on his way back down to Mariposa Beach to investigate another homicide where she was in the mix.

She assumed he would be just as thrilled to see her as she would be about seeing him.

"My bookstore is scheduled to open in a couple days," Dana informed Officer Freddy.

Freddy shrugged. "Your bookstore is an active crime scene, so it will be up to the OIJ to clear it, but I'm afraid it will probably be longer than two days," he said.

Dana's heart sunk.

Mindy put her arm around Dana.

"Come on, Dana, you should go home, there is nothing to gain by staying here."

"Can we leave?" Benny asked Freddy.

He looked at his watch. "Um, yes, sure, go home, but don't leave town. When the detectives arrive, they will want to talk with you two," Freddy said, pointing at Dana and Benny.

Dana's heart sunk even lower.

THIRTEEN

Mindy headed back to her coffee shop while Dana and Benny drove back to Casa Verde in their vehicles. It was six a.m., and the sun was breaking through. It already felt muggy, so it was going to be a hot day as usual in the tropics.

Dana felt terrible. She was still shaken up over finding Barry Shy dead on the bookstore's floor. She felt bad that he was dead. And then Officer Freddy took the keys to her bookstore, so she couldn't have access to her own store until it was cleared by the OIJ.

And if all that weren't bad enough, soon the gossip grape vines in town would be buzzing with the juicy news that Barry Shy was murdered. Inside Dana's bookstore. And that the bookstore's grand opening probably wouldn't happen as planned while the OIJ processed the crime scene... her bookstore. She wanted to cry, but she swallowed hard instead. No point in feeling sorry for herself. Barry Shy was dead, after all, and the police needed to find his killer.

Luckily, it was a fast drive from Ark Row to Casa Verde, so she didn't have to dwell on those thoughts for too long.

She drove up to her front gate with Benny pulling in behind her in his SUV.

As the front gates slowly revealed the lush green landscaping and the jungle-like setting of Casa Verde, she felt better. Those were the images she wanted in her head, not that of Barry Shy's feet sticking out from behind her counter.

She figured the old hippy would haunt her dreams that night, and she actually chuckled. The old pain in the rear would probably get a big kick out of causing an expat merchant to lose sleep from beyond.

She eased in Big Red into the carport as Benny parked in the driveway.

"How are you doing?" he asked, a worried look across his face.

"I've had better days, but I'm doing better than poor Barry," Dana said.

Benny offered a thin smile. "That is true," he said as they walked inside.

Wally came sauntering over to her, giving Benny a quick glare, then he began to rub up and down Dana's leg, purring. He made her smile as she bent down to scratch his ear then pick him up. He was limp like a rag doll as she held him in her arms, petting him.

She looked at Benny, who was smiling. "What?"

"That's one happy, spoiled cat," he said.

"You're just jealous," she said, blushing right away.

He smiled wide but didn't say anything.

That was awkward, Dana thought as she put Wally down and made her way towards the kitchen.

Casa Verde offered breathtaking views of the Pacific Ocean. It sat up on a hillside at the foot of a mountain. Every window in the house offered a view of either the ocean or the jungle.

There was a green, lush footpath that led from her home to

the beach—a leisurely ten-minute walk and she could be swimming in the warm, turquoise waters of the Pacific Ocean.

In the other direction, the pathway led up the mountain, deeper into the jungle where there was a yoga retreat called the Pancha Sabhai Institute. About fifty feet from that was a small bed and breakfast run by Doña Ledia, and beyond that, at the end of the public access footpath, was the private property of a five-star resort, the Tranquil Bay Resort, owned and operated by Gustavo Barca, who was one of Costa Rica's richest people and had a reputation for being a shady developer and landlord. Dana didn't care much for Gustavo Barca, who was the puppet master and financial benefactor of Dana's cousin's legal battles against her.

Barca tried to wrestle ownership of Casa Verde away from her so he could buy it from her cousin in order to expand his ritzy resort. It was common knowledge that he wanted to buy not just Dana's property, but the yoga retreat and the bed and breakfast—that way, he could make the public footpath private and he could extend his snooty resort all the way down to the white-sand Mariposa Beach.

Dana figured if he could, he would buy out the whole town and turn it into a private paradise for his bon vivant guests, but Costa Rica had strict rules that stated that beachfront property could not be privately owned. It was to be open to the public so everyone could enjoy it, not just the rich.

Dana went to her kitchen and poured some water into her red teakettle, which she put on the stove's burner while she opened her tea drawer. She thought about it for a moment and pulled out a couple of mint tea bags.

"Would you like some tea?"

Benny looked at the mint tea. "Not a fan of mint tea. Do you have some Earl Grey or something from the black tea family?"

"I do," she said with a smile as she grabbed a bag of Earl Grey tea for him. "What now?" Dana asked as they waited for the water to boil.

"Not much we can do. We wait for the OIJ to do their thing," Benny replied.

"Did you notice anything odd when you went inside the bookstore?" Dana asked.

"Aside from Barry Shy lying there, no, I didn't. How about you? Did you see anything out of sorts before you found the body?"

"No. I didn't see anything out of place. The front security gate was down and locked. The front door was also locked. But I didn't check the back door. Once I saw those feet sticking out from the counter, I ran back outside."

"Smart thing to do. For all you know, the killer could have still been inside."

It was something that Dana hadn't thought about, and it made her skin crawl and her stomach queasy. She could have been in her store, oblivious that the killer could have still been there. Hiding. Waiting to pounce. She felt relieved that she went with her instinct to get out of there as fast as possible.

The teakettle screamed that the water was boiling, startling her. Benny took over, putting the tea bags in the cups and pouring the hot water while Dana sat there. She felt like she was floating high above, but slowly she felt like she was floating back down to Earth.

"Thank you," she said to Benny as he poured the hot water into her cup.

"You're very welcome. You need to relax if at all possible."

Dana heard him, but the sentiment didn't really register. She was way too shaken up to relax.

"What on earth was Barry up to?" Dana asked.

FOURTEEN

Dana and Benny spent a couple hours talking about what had happened, what could have happened, and what was going to happen to Dana's bookstore.

They tried to change the subject and talk about something else, but that didn't last.

"Well, I'm not leaving tonight as planned, that's for sure," Benny said.

Dana felt bad that he was changing his plans because of what happened in her bookstore, but she felt relieved and happy inside. She didn't want to deal with Detective Picado on her own.

Benny had been such a wonderful friend and attorney since she moved to Mariposa Beach. And it was a bonus that Benny was not only a member of the Costa Rican Bar but also the California Bar, having gone to law school at UC Hastings in Dana's hometown of San Francisco, which she felt was pure serendipity.

Dana had called Ramón Villalobos, Casa Verde's caretaker, and his wife Carmen—both lived in a house on Dana's property

—so she could give him a warning about what was going on, figuring the gossip and the eventual visit by the police would have left him very confused.

To her surprise, about an hour later, Ramón and Carmen stopped by with a pitcher of freshly squeezed mango juice made from the fruits of her own mango trees and a bowl of gallo pinto and corn tortillas.

"Thank you so much, you guys," Dana said, feeling her eyes getting watery.

She invited them inside to join Benny and her, but as usual, they refused.

Benny had explained it was a cultural thing and that it would be difficult for them to do that even though she offered often.

"Don't take it personally," Benny had told her on numerous occasions. "They care for you a lot, but it's just the way they were raised, so it's hard for them to sit down with you to eat."

It was a strange concept for Dana, but she was a guest in their country, so she respected their culture and wishes.

She was just happy they were in her life, taking care of Casa Verde and helping her out so much with everything.

Ramón and Carmen left, and Dana looked at the delicious food and smiled. She wasn't feeling particularly hungry but she appreciated Ramón and Carmen's kind gesture. She grabbed a plate and served herself a spoonful of gallo pinto and a tortilla. Benny did the same then they sat at the kitchen's center island.

Benny was on his second gallo pinto-stuffed tortilla, while Dana was still tearing small pieces of her tortilla and moving gallo pinto around her plate with it. Her mind was on Barry Shy, and it made her lose her appetite.

"I keep going over what Barry could have been doing inside my store. Why he broke in. He didn't have the reputation of a thief, and used books wouldn't really fetch him a fortune, living out in the middle of the jungle as he did. So the only thing that pops in my head is that he was planning some sort of protest or that he was trying to sabotage my grand opening somehow. Why else would he even be in there?

"Maybe he was in cahoots with someone else. They break in. Before they can do their dastardly deed, they argue. It gets physical. Barry winds up dead. His partner in crime panics and hightails it out of there," Dana presented her theory.

Benny filled his glass with more mango juice. "That would explain why Barry's trike was left there. The other person just took off in his own mode of transportation. By car or by foot. It's plausible, I guess," Benny said.

After their meal, Benny took his laptop to the living room to catch up on some work he had to do and to make arrangements with his assistant back in the city, since he wasn't going back as planned.

Dana tidied up the kitchen, and she figured she might as well work on entering more books into the database, since it wasn't like the police would prevent her from opening the bookstore eventually.

She made her way to her den but she found herself googling Barry Shy instead. No matter how deep she thought she was searching, nothing came up. She figured it was a waste of time, with Barry Shy being an old hippy who had lived off the grid in the jungle for more than twenty years, so it was very doubtful he had much of a digital footprint.

She then went farther down the rabbit hole as she googled Benny, coming up with a lot of information about his law practice and several articles about Costa Rican real estate and immigration law. She even found several video interviews on the popular website *CrazyAboutCostaRica.com*. Then she googled herself and found a Facebook post from her ex-husband, Phil Miller and his new fiancée. *Ugh*. She closed her laptop and pushed it away like it was radioactive. She looked at the time on her phone. It was already five thirty p.m.

Wow, the whole day had gone by and not a peep from Detective Picado. She wasn't sure if that was a *no news is good news* type of deal or not.

She emerged from the den. It was already dark outside. For Dana, it was one of the hardest adjustments to living in the tropics. There wasn't a large variation of sunset times like in the United States, where in Northern California the sun would set as early as five p.m. during the winter and as late as eight thirty p.m., even pushing towards nine p.m. during summer.

In Costa Rica, the sun went down between five and five thirty p.m. year-round like clockwork. It didn't matter the month of the year, by six p.m. it was pitch-dark outside, which took some getting used to for a sun-loving California girl like Dana.

Benny was wrapping up a call. He hung up as she walked over to his impromptu office space in her living room. Client folders and loose papers were everywhere.

"Sorry about the mess," he said as he began to tidy up and put the folders into his briefcase.

"No need to apologize. I'm really happy you could work from here. I don't want to deal with Picado on my own."

"I don't blame you. I'm actually surprised we haven't heard from the police at all since this morning."

"Maybe Picado won't show up today, which would be fine with me. I want to know what's going on, but I'm not keen on dealing with him at all," Dana said.

"It's almost six, so you just might get your wish." As soon as Benny said that, Dana's phone rang. It was Officer Freddy.

"Are you at home?"

"Yes."

"Is Mr. Campos there?"

"Yes."

"Good. Detectives Picado and Rojas are on their way to Casa Verde to talk to you both."

Dang it.

She hung up.

"He's on his way, isn't he?"

"We jinxed it."

A few minutes later, she opened the front gate for the detectives.

"They're *here*," Dana said like the girl in the *Poltergeist* movie. Benny laughed.

She found it appropriate that it was dark and ominous outside when he arrived.

Picado walked in with his partner, Detective Gabriela Rojas, who had also worked on the murder case of Dana's cousin.

Dana felt a bit of relief at seeing Detective Rojas. She didn't know if it was part of the bad cop, good cop routine, but Rojas had treated her kindly, whereas Picado was rude and accusatory, and it didn't seem like that had changed as Picado glared at Dana with a peeved expression on his face that made her angry.

But she tried to put her best foot forward, so she offered the detectives something to drink anyway. Picado waved her off dismissively without speaking a word or making eye contact. Rojas smiled and shook her head. "No, thank you."

Dana, Benny, and the two detectives sat in the living room. Dana had bought a beautiful living room set: a couch, loveseat, and oversized chair, all matching in her favorite color for home decor, red.

Dana and Benny sat on the couch. Picado sat in the middle of the love chair, and Rojas sat on the single chair.

Picado pulled out a pocket notebook that reminded Dana of the reporter notebooks she used to carry back in her days as a print journalist in the states.

Detective Rojas placed her iPhone on the table. "If you don't mind, I'm going to record the interview."

Dana looked at Benny, as her attorney, not friend in that moment. "That's fine," he said.

Picado sighed heavily and sat forward at the edge of the chair. "It occurred to me on the way over here that I can't recall of a murder being committed in Mariposa Beach during my fifteen years on the job, and now, in the span of a few months, right after you moved into town, there are two murders and you figure prominently in both of them," Picado said as he pulled out a pen. He smirked and sat back on the chair, crossing his legs as he flipped open his notepad. He looked like a smug psychiatrist ready to get personal.

Dana didn't say anything, trying hard not to let him get under her skin, but to her surprise, Benny spoke up.

"What's that supposed to mean?" he asked, sounding annoyed.

"It means that the last time I was in Mariposa Beach was due to the murder of Ms. Kirkpatrick's cousin, and now I'm back to investigate a murder of Mr. Barry Shy, who happened to be killed inside of Ms. Kirkpatrick's bookstore. I find that curious. Don't you find that curious?"

"I do not," Benny replied.

"I find it to be a nightmare," Dana said.

Picado scribbled on his notepad.

"Just do your job without making innuendos about Dana," Benny snapped.

"I *am* doing my job. So, Ms. Kirkpatrick, did you know the victim?"

"Yes," Dana replied, remembering Benny's advice that when talking to the police, the less you said, the better, keeping answers to yes and no being the ideal response.

"Did you know Mr. Shy, Mr. Campos?"

"Yes. Everyone around town knew Barry Shy."

"Was Mr. Shy working for you or helping you with your bookstore in some capacity?"

Dana snorted with laughter, which she immediately regretted for being inappropriate, all things considered.

"Sorry. I don't mean to laugh. But Barry Shy wasn't exactly nice to me. As you probably know by now, he wanted to shut me down before I even opened my front door." *Oops, there goes my yes and no answers.*

"Why is that?" Picado asked.

"He didn't like new businesses coming to town. He said expats like me and the business I was opening were ruining Mariposa Beach and turning it into Rodeo Drive."

Picado silently scribbled some more on his notebook.

"Any idea why he would be in your bookstore?"

"No. And he didn't have permission to be there, that's for sure, so no, I don't know what he was doing there or how he got in. Did you figure out how he got in? My security gate out front was securely locked without signs of tampering," Dana said.

Picado studied her for a moment in awkward silence until Detective Gabriela Rojas spoke up. "It looks like he climbed in through the back window, which was broken."

"That window is like ten feet from the ground and has metal bars," Dana said.

"They probably used a ladder or some other way to climb up to the window, then they cut the bars with what appears to have been a hacksaw of some sorts. We haven't located a ladder or a hacksaw, so whoever killed Mr. Shy must have taken those items with him," Rojas said.

"The forensic investigator team just arrived from San José, and they'll be able to provide more details on that," Picado said.

"That is strange. Barry had a bad reputation in town for being a loudmouth and confrontational with everybody, but he wasn't a thief who broke into and entered a business like that," Benny said.

"You never know what anyone is capable of," Picado said, looking over at Dana.

What a jerk. Dana stared back at him until he looked down into his notebook and started scribbling again.

"Is the body..." Dana didn't want to finish the question. "Is it still there?"

"Yes. Once the crime scene investigators are finished, the body will be transported to the medical examiner in San José."

"I hate to be crass, but I have a bookstore grand opening in less than forty-eight hours. When will I be able to get back into my store?"

Picado grunted something inaudible then said, "That entire location is a crime scene, so I'm afraid it will be off limits for several days, maybe even a week or more."

Dana closed her eyes as Benny protested, to no avail. Picado promptly cut him off.

"Your little bookstore opening is not my concern. It's a crime scene now, and you won't be able to access it until I tell you that you can. You'll just have to reschedule your grand opening. I have a killer to catch," Picado said, standing up.

"You know the drill from the last time. Don't leave town without my permission. And don't go into your bookstore until I release it as a crime scene. I'll be in touch. We'll let ourselves out," he said as he turned around and walked towards the front door. Rojas gave Dana a sympathetic smile as she followed Picado out.

Dana and Benny stood there, taken aback by the abrupt ending to the interview.

"I know he has a really important job to do, but he just drives me crazy. What. A. Jerk," Dana said, seething.

FIFTEEN

Despite everything that was going on, Dana was excited. Her best friend, Courtney Lowe, was coming for a visit from San Francisco.

It was supposed to be a surprise to celebrate the opening of the bookstore, but after Dana told her about the dead body she found inside her bookstore and how the police had put the kibosh on her grand opening, Courtney just fessed up that she was planning to show up the day before her grand opening to surprise her.

Dana was touched. "You don't have to," she told her over a WhatsApp video call.

"I wouldn't have missed the opening of your store for anything," Courtney said. "And now I'm really glad I'm going down there so you don't have to go through this alone."

It got her mind off the bad news, and she couldn't help but feel excited that Courtney was coming for a visit.

Courtney Lowe had been Dana's best friend since they met as college students at Berkeley. Courtney went into the public relations field right out of college, while Dana became a journalist.

After years of reporting for the dying print media, which meant salary freezes, the forced transformation of journalists into bloggers and social media wranglers, and the constant threat of layoffs always looming, Dana had enough, and it was Courtney who helped her find a high-paying job in public relations. Dana enjoyed the money and perks, but she felt like a fish out of water, working in the millennial hipster enclave of SoMa —South of Market—located just south of Market Street in San Francisco.

The job paid well but she hated it, so after her divorce and when she got a chance to move to Mariposa Beach, she jumped at it.

Courtney had come down with Dana on that first trip to Mariposa Beach to help her get settled in, and had been a rock for her when dealing with her cousin's lawsuit and death.

Even though they were a thousand miles from each other, they texted every day and video called each other often.

But Dana missed seeing her friend in the flesh, so she was excited that she was coming down even if her planned surprise had been ruined and the visit would be muddled by the ongoing investigation of Barry Shy's murder in her bookstore.

The day after finding a dead body, the police didn't have any updates they would share with her, and her bookstore was still off limits to her.

The grand opening, which was supposed to be in twenty-four hours, was now on hold until the police were done with their investigation.

Although that was hard for Dana to deal with and it made her feel down, that all changed with the arrival of Courtney into town. It was a boost of happiness.

Dana drove up to the tiny Nosara Municipal Airport, which consisted of just one landing strip. Calling it an airport was generous. There wasn't a control tower or anything like that, just one concrete runway and a small open-air concrete building that was called the terminal but looked more like a big bus shelter than an airport terminal.

She was looking into the sky when she saw a little single-engine airplane approach for landing. She smiled, knowing how much Courtney hated flying in Captain Junior's puddle jumper. He made the trip from San José to Nosara three times a week.

Captain Junior landed the plane masterfully as always. He taxied down the small tarmac and stopped right in front of the terminal, killing the engine. A few moments later, the door opened as the foot ladder unfolded onto the tarmac.

Dana laughed out loud when she saw a pale-faced Courtney jump out of the airplane as if she were gasping for air.

On the ground, Courtney regained her color as she ran towards Dana, and the two friends hugged each other.

"How was the trip?" Dana asked, grinning.

"Oy. Don't ask. I swore that I would never fly in that tin can in the sky again. I should have listened to myself and driven instead."

"I would have picked you up in San José."

"It was supposed to be a surprise visit, and I had already made the flight arrangements with Captain Junior, so here I am."

Courtney smiled, and the two friends hugged again.

"Doña Dana, how are you?" an excited Captain Junior asked as he approached, giving her a hug.

The tico culture was much more into hugging and cheek kissing than most Americans, like Dana, were comfortable with, but she was getting used to it. It was part of the culture, so she didn't want to be rude. When in Rome, and all that.

She exchanged pleasantries for a minute with the pilot and owner of Tropic Air who was decked out in his usual captain's uniform, down to a pair of epaulets on his shoulders and his captain's cap. He took pride in his job and his two-plane airline.

They said goodbye to the captain, and Dana and Courtney walked elbow-to-elbow towards Big Red. A nice advantage of the rural airport was that there was no customs or immigration to go through, you just got out of the airplane and walked to your car.

Courtney laughed when she saw Dana's Jeep. "Big Red, I've actually missed the little bugger." Dana smiled, knowing that Courtney was just as afraid of her little Jeep as she was of Captain Junior's airplane, especially when she took it off-roading.

Courtney tossed her carry-on suitcase in the back of Big Red and climbed into the passenger seat as Dana got behind the wheel.

"Jeez, Dana, what is going on down here?" Courtney asked as Dana fired up the Jeep.

"I don't know, but first there was Roy's murder and now Barry Shy is killed in my bookstore... people in town are going to think I bring bad luck of the worst kind."

Dana put the Jeep in first and took off down a dirt road. She put the gear into second and then into third as she drove Big Red onto the paved road towards the coast.

It was warm and sunny, so Big Red's soft top was rolled back so they could feel the warm wind and sun on their faces. Courtney was prepared for that, so she had put on a San Francisco Giants baseball hat on which she had to hold at times with her hand in case the wind took it off her head.

"You said on WhatsApp that the dead man was harassing you? So what was that about?"

"He was a bit odd, and that's me being nice. His nickname in town was the Unabomber because he looked and acted like Ted Kaczynski. He lived out of town in a wooden shack without electricity, spouting hatred against technology, and he harassed just about everyone in town at one time or another. I was just his project du jour because I was new in town and was opening up the bookstore."

Courtney bit her lip. "Yikes."

"Oh, it gets worse. Remember that detective that investigated Roy's murder, Jorge Picado?"

"Of course, Mr. Preventive Detention," Courtney said, referring to the legal practice in Costa Rica where suspects could be held without being charged for months while the police investigated. Picado had threatened them both with preventive detention during the murder investigation of Dana's cousin, which had left a lasting impression.

Just like with law enforcement, there were a lot of differences between the United States and Costa Rican legal system.

Costa Rica followed the French legal system where basically you were considered guilty until proven innocent. There was no double jeopardy, so prosecutors could keep trying to nail you over and over if they wanted. And there was no jury of your peers, so cases were decided by judges, and the police could hold you in preventive detention for months without charging you with a crime.

"Don't tell me he's working this case too."

"Yup," Dana said, flooring the accelerator.

"Okay, I know you're upset, but slow down, please."

Dana smiled then suddenly shifted Big Red down to its second gear and steered wide to the right in order to avoid a pothole the size of Texas.

Courtney was holding on to the passenger-side bar for dear life. "I swear that sucker was there last time. But now it's even bigger. They really don't fix potholes, do they?" Courtney asked.

Dana laughed. "Nope. Makes driving more interesting."

Courtney white-knuckled the sidebar grip of the Jeep for the entire thirty-minute drive from Nosara to Mariposa Beach.

Back in Casa Verde, Dana handed Courtney a chilled coconut that had been stripped of its husk and had its top hacked off by a machete, with a bamboo straw placed into the hole. Dana had switched to the reusable bamboo straws after reading how the plastic straws that ended up in the ocean could cause great harm to marine life like dolphins.

"Oh, I missed these," Courtney said, eagerly accepting the cold coconut and taking a large drink of the delicious sweet juice from the straw. "Mmm. The real deal. It sure beats the coconut water you get back home from a carton. And I bet this didn't cost eight bucks a pop."

"I could buy Don Flaudio's daily supply of real coconuts for that amount," Dana teased.

Don Flaudio was the old man who sold the coconuts from the back of an old, rusted pickup truck on the side of the road.

"So how are things back in San Francisco?"

"Oh, same old. The tech bros and hipsters clip-clop through a pee-stained and needle-riddled sidewalk to get their avocado toast and drip coffee."

Dana laughed.

"You don't miss it?"

"Well, not when you put it like that." They both laughed out loud.

Dana would be lying if she said she didn't miss the big-city life from time to time. And for all its big-city problems, San Francisco was a beautiful city by the bay. But she was happy in her new home. The change of pace from high speed to a crawl suited her well, which actually surprised her a lot.

"And how's Benny?" Courtney grinned.

"Fine. You can ask him yourself when we go out to dinner tonight."

"And..."

"And, what?"

"Don't play coy with me, missy, when are you changing the status of your relationship with that cutie pie from friend to lover?" Courtney asked, pronouncing *lover* as *lov-ah* for dramatic effect.

"Ew, at least say boyfriend, not lover, but honestly, I haven't had much time to think about that. I've been busy getting the bookstore ready, and he spends most of his time in the city with his legal practice, so it's just best to keep things as they are. We've become great friends."

"Too busy. Sure. Well, you can't fight off that chemistry between you two forever."

"Okay, Oprah, interview over, can we change the subject?"

"Are you really liking it down here? Like really?"

"I do. Of course there have been times when it was hard making the adjustment, being the new expat in town, and there are cultural differences that take some getting used to, but it's been starting to feel more and more like home, and opening up my bookstore was giving me a wonderful sense of purpose. I felt like I could give back to the community, and now I don't even know when I'll be able to open." Dana could feel her eyes getting watery.

"The police didn't give a timeframe to work with?"

Dana sighed audibly. "Nope. Detective Picado was adamant it might take days or weeks. He doesn't care about my business. And I can't wait that long to keep my bookstore in limbo after I've put in time and money into it. But I come off like a jerk for being impatient about this whole situation, since a man is dead and his killer is still out there on the loose, so Picado does have an important job to do."

"Of course," Courtney said.

"I just wish he did it faster," Dana said with a grin.

SIXTEEN

Benny arrived at the house a couple hours after Dana got back from her airport run with Courtney.

He had sent Dana a text that he was on his way. She texted him "come on up," which meant they were chilling upstairs on the veranda.

A few minutes later, they heard the tires crunching on the gravel driveway.

Dana got up from her big, comfy patio chair and looked over the railing. She waved down at Benny and shouted, "Come on up," repeating her text message verbally.

"Come on up," Courtney repeated in her best Mae West impression, which was actually quite terrible.

"You sound like Wally trying to cough up a hairball."

Wally had been curled up against Dana, and had taken over her chair the moment she got up to look over the railing. He looked at her, and she swore he gave her a dirty look for the little insult.

"Ooh, Wally didn't like that," Courtney said, laughing.

Dana also laughed, then she plopped on her chair, giving Wally a brief warning. "Scoot over, mister." He meowed his displeasure, jumped off the chair, and then joined Courtney on the chaise lounge.

"Traitor!" Dana hissed at Wally, then broke out laughing.

They were waiting for Benny to make his way upstairs when Dana's phone buzzed. She looked at the screen and said with some dread in her voice, "It's Detective Picado." Courtney looked at her nervously as Dana took the call.

Benny arrived as she was talking to him on her phone. Courtney mouthed "Detective Picado" at him and he gave the same nervous look that Courtney had given Dana.

They spoke for several minutes. Benny and Courtney only heard Dana's side of the conversation, which seemed to have been cut short over and over by the detective, since her side of the conversation consisted of "Yes, but... Why... I need to... Stop interrupting..."

Dana hung up the phone. Benny and Courtney's puzzled faces were looking at her.

"He is so obnoxious," Dana said, sounding exasperated.

"What did he want?" Benny asked.

"He wants me to go to the bookstore in order to see if anything is missing. He's given me fifteen minutes inside. I can't remove anything, just take a look at everything—including my book inventory—to see if anything is missing."

"When?" Benny asked Dana.

"In one hour."

"Whoa. Okay, I'll go with you," Courtney said.

"No. He was very adamant that I'm the only one allowed inside. He even mentioned you by name," Dana said, looking at Benny.

They debated on that for a bit. "At the very least let me drive you. I'll wait in the car," Benny said.

"Me too," Courtney added.

"No, thank you, I don't want to give that jerk any more

ammunition to hate on me more than he already does. I'll just run down there and do as he asks. It won't take me long. I have everything cataloged and entered into my database, so if any books were taken, I'll know rather quickly thanks to Bucky's software."

Benny and Courtney acquiesced. "I have some of my ceviche you like so much at home. I made it fresh last night, so it should be perfect right now, so I'll run out to get it, and we can have a little feast when you get back," Benny said.

Dana smiled. "That would be wonderful."

She headed outside and fired up Big Red.

Dana pulled into Ark Row's small parking lot. Tomás, the security guard, was there, and he greeted her sheepishly as he began to apologize profusely for not being there when she needed him.

"Don't worry, Tomás, you can't stay here twenty-four seven. Stuff happens."

She walked slowly towards her bookstore. *Can I even refer it to as my bookstore if it's never been open for business?*

She saw an old, beat-up white pickup parked in front. She wasn't sure if that was an OIJ unmarked vehicle or not. Usually Picado and Rojas drove around in a sedan.

There wasn't any police presence out front. She expected to see a uniformed police officer like Freddy Sanchez guarding the entrance, but no one was there. It was eerily quiet.

The yellow tape was still there, but some of it had been cut in order to access the front door. She looked around, and there was no one there. She reached for the front door, and just as she was about to turn the knob, the door flung open, making her flinch.

Detective Gabriela Rojas popped out from inside and smiled. "Hi, sorry, didn't mean to startle you."

"It's fine. I'm just a bit jumpy since all this started."

"That's completely understandable. Thank you for coming."

"Your partner made it sound like I didn't have a choice."

Rojas shrugged. She knew the senior detective was a handful. "Come on, he's waiting inside."

Dana went inside and looked around her baby. She hadn't been inside since she had discovered Barry Shy's body.

Seeing Picado standing there behind *her* counter, next to the covered-up cash register, made her angry. *That's supposed to be my spot behind the counter, not anyone else's—even you, Mr. Hotshot detective.*

Dana was soon distracted from her dislike of the detective when an eerie feeling took over, causing the small hairs on her arms to stand up and for her to shiver even though it was warm inside. A man was killed in her bookstore. Right down there where Picado was standing is where she found the body. Right there.

"Ms. Kirkpatrick," Picado barked as Rojas nudged her, causing her to snap out of her trance. It dawned on her that she must have drifted away and hadn't heard Picado speaking to her the first time.

"Sorry, what did you say?"

Picado sighed and rolled his eyes. "Do you have your inventory computerized?"

"Um..." She looked at Picado's face, which in her mind was coming in and out of focus, something she chalked up to the stress of everything that was going on.

"Well, do you? Yes or no. It's a simple question," Picado barked out.

"Um, yes, I do have everything catalogued in my bookselling software."

"Can you print or email your inventory to me?" Rojas asked.

"Sure. Why?"

Rojas explained, "We need to determine if anything has been stolen, which is why you're here, but if you have your inventory in the computer, then it will make sure we don't over-look something."

"You think Barry was stealing books?"

"What was the value of these books?" Picado asked.

"It's a used-book store. Cheap. Definitely nothing to get killed over."

"Any computers or electronic equipment you kept here?" Rojas asked.

"No. Just that cash register, which only works when I dock my iPad to it, so it's useless in that state."

Picado and Rojas exchanged acknowledging glances as if they had been trying to figure out how the modern-looking point-of-sale cash register worked.

"And there is no money inside?"

Dana nodded as she began to look around her store. "No. As you're aware, I haven't even opened for business yet."

"So there is nothing that would be of value to a burglar."

"No..." Dana replied, trailing off as she looked around.

She looked at the beautiful bookshelves Benny and Rodri had made and began to go through the books on them. She took out her iPad from her purse and flicked it on and tapped on Bucky's bookselling app. A graphic of a closed book loaded, then the book opened as a blue morpho butterfly flew out from between the pages of the book and floated across the screen before vanishing.

It made her want to cry, thinking about her bookstore and its now doomed grand opening.

Dana checked all the books on the shelf against her book-selling software under the watchful eye of Detective Picado.

She would scan the barcode on the spine of the book with her iPhone's camera and a second later there would be a bleep and all the pertinent information about that book would get pulled up.

"What's the name of the software program?" Picado asked, sounding impressed.

"It's custom software a friend of mine from Silicon Valley created for me."

"Is the data stored in the cloud?" Rojas asked.

Dana nodded, not saying anything as she scanned another book.

"We'll need access to it as well as a full copy of your product database so we can check what's here to pin down what was stolen."

"I already told you, I don't think anything is missing."

"We still need that data."

"Okay, I'll email it to you," Dana said, looking at Detective Rojas.

Dana arrived back home to Casa Verde about an hour later. It was dark out.

Benny and Courtney greeted her with hugs and smiles.

"That was a long fifteen minutes," Courtney said.

"Once I got there, he seemed to be a bit more relaxed, and he wanted me to be thorough, so I guess he changed his mind about only letting me be there for fifteen minutes."

"Anything missing?" Benny asked.

"Nada. And after an hour with Picado, I need a drink," Dana said as she beelined to the kitchen.

On the kitchen center island was a large white bowl filled with homemade ceviche that Benny had made.

He explained that his ceviche was made using raw corvina —a firm white fish popular in Costa Rica, like sea bass back in the states—and small shrimp.

The fish was diced into cubes then tossed into a bowl with the shrimp, where it was marinated in lime juice, which cooked it. He also included chopped red bell peppers, onions, cilantro, minced jalapeños, salt, pepper, and the secret ingredient which Benny insisted made it a tico ceviche: ginger ale.

The bowl was then tightly sealed with plastic wrap and put in the refrigerator overnight.

It was then served with saltine crackers, sliced avocado, and splashed with Salsa Lizano and hot sauce in case the jalapeños didn't provide enough of a kick.

Dana smiled at the sight. "Oh, yum, thank you," she said, scooping a spoonful of ceviche onto a soda cracker. She splashed Salsa Lizano onto the ceviche to make it even more of a Costa Rican dish. She skipped the hot sauce, since she thought the jalapeños made the dish hot enough for her palate.

After a few soda crackers loaded with ceviche and a few sips of chilled Sauvignon blanc, she was feeling much better and ready to tell them about her meeting with the OIJ detectives.

"There isn't that much to tell, really. Nothing was missing. Like Freddy told us, Barry broke in through the back window. It had those metal bars and was high enough that I figured it was foolproof against burglary. The police say that Barry parked his trike out back, used a ladder to climb up to the window and hacksawed the metal bars so he could break the window and climb inside," Dana said.

"You know, Barry Shy was a sanctimonious twit, but the man was honest as the day is long. He's lived down here for over thirty years and he's never been known to steal anything. I can't imagine he would break into your bookstore to burglarize it. Besides, he weighs like a buck fifty, and he's in his sixties and frail. That takes some serious burglar skills, and I don't see Barry possessing that skillset," Benny commented.

"That's why the police suspect he had an accomplice, and it's that person that killed Barry for reasons unknown," Dana said.

"To steal used books. Doesn't make any sense."

"I told Picado that he was going on and on about how he wanted to shut me down, so perhaps he was there to sabotage my grand opening."

"I still can't see him going through all that work. If he were going to shut anything down, he would target the real estate office or one of the McMansions being built around here recently. Not a bookstore. He was all bark and no bite. He threatened just about everyone in town all the time. Myself included," Benny said.

"Every dog has his day," Dana said. She laughed.

"What's so funny?" Courtney asked.

"Well, it's ironic. Regardless of what he was up to, he did succeed in shutting me down."

SEVENTEEN

Dana knew it was going to be a rough day. It was the day of her planned grand opening of the bookstore, which was put on hold by the police.

Instead of the planned balloons and streamers, the front door had yellow police tape forbidding entry. And to top it off, she hadn't been given any indication on when she might be able to open. Tomorrow? A few days? Next month? If Detective Picado knew, he wasn't sharing that tidbit of information with her.

The only thing that was certain was that all the planning, promotions, and advertisements she had prepared for the big day would be going to waste.

She shuddered at the thought of people showing up for the grand opening only to be met by crime scene tape. News traveled fast in the coastal rumor vine, but not everyone was part of it. Perhaps someone came across one of her ads or flyers and hadn't heard about the dead man found in the bookstore, so they made the trip down to find the bookstore closed and being labeled as a crime scene.

Dana had called Detective Picado several times, asking him

if she couldn't open her bookstore as planned, if he would allow her five minutes to hang up a sign on the front door explaining what was going on. He didn't return her call, and she didn't have her key, so she was locked out of her own business.

Dana was happy Courtney was in town, because she would have probably spent all day in bed with Wally if not for her friend being there.

Well, since she wasn't going to hide under the covers in bed all day, she came up with a Plan B. She got out of bed as Wally scattered away. She showered and got dressed, then went downstairs and began to pack some items into a box.

"What are you up to?" Courtney asked as she came down the stairs, yawning.

"I can't just sit here all day thinking about potential customers that are planning to attend the grand opening only to be greeted by yellow police tape. So I'm going to have a little sidewalk sale."

"I'm sure Picado is going to love that," Courtney said facetiously.

"I'll set up right across from the bookstore on the sidewalk. I'll make sure not to block the walkway. I already spoke with Big Mike and the other merchants, and they're okay with it. Big Mike loved the idea, since it would bring people to Ark Row. It's a public sidewalk. I have the okay of my Ark Row neighbors, and I'll make sure to keep the sidewalk clear, so Picado can go fly a kite."

"Oh jeez, Dana, you're poking the bear again. But well, let's do this."

Dana appreciated her support because she knew Courtney had reservations about what Dana was doing—heck, so did she, but the reason was that Picado scared the living daylights out of Courtney ever since he threatened Dana and Courtney with preventive detention arrest during the investigation of Dana's cousin's murder. They both had seen enough episodes of *Locked up Abroad* to be terrified about what could happen, but Dana was going through with it as she put the final touches to the signage for the event that she was calling a "Pop-up Bookstore."

Courtney put her excellent drawing skills to use and she put together a beautiful signage indicating that bookstore's new grand opening was in a TBD status. She made sure to express condolences for the well-known expat that was killed in Dana's bookstore, a thought that didn't fail to send shivers up and down Dana's spine.

Bless her, Dana thought as she stopped at Mindy's Coffee and Bagels to pick up a special order that Mindy had whipped up for Dana's impromptu pop-up.

She had contributed two dozen banana-walnut muffins and a one-hundred-ounce carafe of her freshly brewed dark roast coffee. Light coffee and decaf drinkers were out of luck.

"You are wonderful," Dana said, hugging Mindy and waving at Leo, who was in the kitchen.

"I'm so glad you're here for her, Courtney," Mindy said, smiling at Courtney.

"The plan was to be here for the special day, so I wish that were still the case, but I'm glad to be here for her nevertheless."

"What's the word?" Dana asked Mindy, since her coffee shop was like Grand Central Station when it came to gossip and innuendo.

Mindy gave her a stiff look as she bit the inside of her cheek.

"That bad, huh?"

"Oh, honey, don't worry about those folks flapping their gums about things they have no clue about."

"What are they saying?"

"Just about the odds of two murders happening so close to each other."

"And how I'm at the center of both, I suppose."

"Ignore it, honey!"

"Bunch of superstitious mumbo jumbo," Leo shouted from the kitchen.

Dana and Courtney loaded up the muffins and coffee carafe into Big Red, and Dana drove as slowly as a blue-haired lady to avoid the dips and potholes in the road while they drove the short distance between the coffee shop and the bookstore crime scene.

Dana and Courtney were setting up their table with a plate of muffins, coffee cups, and the dozen paperbacks Dana brought along to sell. It wasn't about making money—she wouldn't—but just to show people she was around and the bookstore would eventually open.

"Hey, Courtney, you're back in town, pura vida," Big Mike said, smiling. He had met Courtney and Dana when they were hanging out on the beach the first time Courtney had been to Costa Rica, and he gave them surfing lessons.

He turned his attention towards Dana. "This is a great idea, girl."

"I just couldn't sit home, being that today was supposed to be the grand opening."

"Yeah, that's a real bummer, man," Big Mike said, eyeing the goodies. "Are these free?"

Dana smiled and said they were.

"Awesome, thanks," Big Mike said as he grabbed a muffin and poured himself a cup of coffee.

"You're in your store all day, have you seen or heard anything about what's been going on here with the police?" Dana asked.

Big Mike shook his head as he took a bite of the muffin.

"Man, Mindy makes good muffins," he said, swallowing. "Detective Rojas asked me some questions, if I had seen or heard anything suspicious, but I told her I hadn't. They did ask for the video from my security cameras on the day of the murder, so I gave them that. But haven't heard anything since then. All I can tell you is what I've seen. The forensics people were in your bookstore for hours. Then Picado dropped by and asked me more questions. That dude is wound tight."

"What kind of questions was Picado asking?"

"Oh, about you, your store, and if I'd ever seen you and Barry Shy together and if you two had a beef."

Dana bit her lip. Big Mike picked up on the worry that flashed across her face.

"Oh, man, don't worry, Dana. I told Picado straight up that Barry Shy had a beef with everyone in town, myself included. The list of suspects that had motive to kill him could fill an Agatha Christie novel."

Dana laughed. "*Murder On The Orient Express* is one of the books I'll have for sale today, and in that book, spoiler alert, every one of the passengers was the killer."

Big Mike chuckled. "Well I'm right next door if you need anything," he said as he made his way back to his store.

EIGHTEEN

Dana and Courtney spent three hours manning the table. It seemed just about everyone that stopped by knew what had happened to Barry Shy in her store, but there were a few folks that arrived from out of town because of her flyers. They were surprised to find the bookstore closed and its front gate adorned with yellow police tape and a paper notice with OIJ signage posted up on the front gate, indicating that the bookstore was a crime scene and anyone entering would be subject to arrest. They were the reason she set up her pop-up store.

The OIJ verbiage alone was enough to make people think that Dana had done something criminal. She wanted to be out there smiling, handing out free muffins and coffee, selling used books like it was a garage sale. She wanted to show them she wasn't locked up away in jail or mixed up in some shady dealings.

So she manned her table, handing out cups of coffee and muffins, shaking hands like a politician and accepting hugs from concerned locals, and even talking about books with a few of them.

At one point there were several people hovering around the

table and a few others loitering nearby, trying hard to look like they were not eavesdropping or trying to peek inside the store.

She hadn't gotten the chance to remove the tarp she had hung up to cover the windows, which she had planned to remove during the grand-opening reveal, so that added to an aura of mystery as to what was going on inside.

Doña Ledia Wallace, the owner of the bed and breakfast up the pathway from Dana's property, showed up.

They had only met once, and she hadn't been very friendly towards Dana, who didn't know why. The owner of the bed and breakfast had looked at her with a noticeably stern visage and said "Sorry, no walk-ins, we're full." Even after Dana had explained she wasn't a guest but her neighbor, there to introduce herself and say hello, Doña Ledia practically shooed her away, saying she was too busy with guests, and that had been the last she had seen of her until the day of her pop-up.

Dana had made the effort to be neighborly, so she was fine with that. She had done the same thing at the Pancha Sabhai Institute, a world-class yoga retreat established fifteen years ago by a well-known yoga teacher and guru from upstate New York who went by the name of Jai Das but his real name was Vincent Marino. Jai had been the complete opposite of Doña Ledia. He welcomed Dana to their "little patch of land" and invited her to attend one of his events, for free. He seemed thrilled that she had dropped by to introduce herself as the new neighbor.

Being from San Francisco, Dana was used to enlightenment-seeking people like Jai Das.

Doña Ledia walked up to Dana's table set-up and looked around. "You're not supposed to sell on the sidewalk without a permit," she said with contempt.

"I didn't know that, thanks for letting me know," Dana said smiling.

Doña Ledia stood there for a moment or two but Dana wasn't moving.

"Have a muffin, they're delicious," Dana said.

"No, thank you," she said curtly and walked away.

And now, as if having Doña Ledia's antics weren't bad enough, the annoying tourist book collector Chris Smith who had been practically stalking her came barreling through a few folks that had congregated by the table and were chatting with Dana and Courtney.

He grabbed a muffin and filled a cup of coffee without asking or thanking Dana. "Any updates from the police?" he asked as he chewed on a muffin.

His rudeness knows no bounds, Dana thought, watching him scarf down the muffin in three bites.

"No updates," Dana said.

He took a look at the books she had on the table, but they must have not interested him. He grabbed a second muffin and walked away.

Courtney looked at Dana, puzzled.

"I'll tell you later about that guy," Dana said rolling her eyes.

Just then the Gossip Brigade of septuagenarian and octogenarian busybodies showed up. Dana smiled. She found them endearing and annoying all at once. The entire brigade was there: Doña Amada, Doña Chilla, Doña Luz, and Doña Marta, a group of widows that had known each other for over fifty years and bickered and argued like an old married couple. Dana figured if anyone had any updates on the case, it would be these ladies.

They came on like a hurricane. Loud. Arguing with each other. Hugging and kissing Dana and telling her how sorry they were that her grand opening was ruined. Then they complained about what a royal pain Barry Shy had been in life and how Detective Picado was just as bad. But they didn't have any new information to share with her. The Gossip Brigade had come up empty.

Freddy Sanchez, the motocross-riding police officer, showed up twenty minutes later saying that someone—Dana was sure "someone" was Doña Ledia—had called the police to complain about an illegal sidewalk sale.

"What's going on?" Freddy asked suspiciously as he eyed the gathering.

Dana explained what she was doing there and assured him that she was not interfering with the OIJ's crime scene, or as Dana preferred calling it, *my bookstore.*

Freddy looked around and checked on the yellow police tape. Since everything seemed in order, he nodded at Dana his okay with what she was doing.

"Any updates on the case?" Dana asked.

"Not that I'm aware. Detective Picado went up to San José yesterday to go over the findings with the forensic team and the medical examiner."

That explained why he didn't come around to force her to leave, Dana thought. Good timing.

After about twenty minutes of guarding the scene and after having eaten two muffins and downed two cups of coffee, Officer Freddy left, thanking her for the muffins and coffee, but warning her to keep out of the bookstore. He jumped on his motocross bike and roared away.

An hour later, all the muffins were gone, as was most of the coffee, so Dana and Courtney decided to wrap it up.

She sold only two paperbacks. Sue Grafton's *"K" is for Killer*—and no, the irony was not lost on Dana or the customer as the awkward transaction was made—and James Michener's

Caribbean, one of his thoroughly enjoyable doorstopper novels.

But more importantly to her was that she was there to greet visitors, even the annoying ones like the rude bibliophile tourist and the snotty Doña Ledia.

She was able to let them know in person that she would be opening her bookstore as soon as the OIJ allowed it.

She was also able to chat and bond further with her Ark Row neighbors. Dana had gotten to know Big Mike well since she had moved to town. His surf shop was located next to hers. On the other side was an empty retail store. Next to the empty location was Pacific Realty. Next to Big Mike's Surf Shop was Gavilán Tours, owned by Bill Kingman, an expat from Florida who owns the *Gavilán* fishing boat. He arranged deep-sea fishing trips for tourists. He had stopped by to introduce himself and to share his own Barry Shy horror story with Dana.

"Barry hated me. He was a militant vegan and didn't like that I took out tourists to go fishing for marlin, snook, and sailfish. He said I was complicit in a fish genocide. He was quite the character."

At the end of Ark Row was a small jiujitsu and CrossFit gym owned by Frank Reyes, a Costa Rican martial arts expert who had represented Costa Rica in the 1984 Olympics in Los Angeles. He didn't earn a medal in judo, but he made the country proud, being one of the first Costa Ricans to make it to the Olympics. He was short, with a shaved head, and soft-spoken. His voice reminded Dana of Mike Tyson's voice. But like Tyson, he gave off an aura that let you know that he was not a man to be messed with. Dana had worked out at his CrossFit gym, so she knew Frank well, and she was happy that he had stopped by to let her know he had her support. He also shared his story about being harassed by Barry Shy—martial arts expert or not, Barry got in his face for teaching violence. "Obviously you don't know anything about the martial arts if you think it promotes violence," Frank would tell Barry Shy.

At the other end of Ark Row was Ernesto and Dora Castro's corner shop—a small grocery store, known as pulperías in Costa Rica.

Dora came over to say hello, explaining that Ernesto was manning the store, so he couldn't come. Dana had shopped in their pulpería plenty of times since moving to town. It was a quick trip from Casa Verde when she needed a gallon of milk or Diet Coke. Dora didn't seem to be as warm and friendly as she had in the past. Dana wrote it off as the circumstances surrounding her arrival to town and now being at the center of two different homicides might cause anyone to be a bit stand-offish around her.

Hopefully when the murder was solved, she would come around, Dana hoped.

Dana and Courtney climbed into Big Red. "I'm glad we did this," she said.

"It turned out well. Good thinking. Sorry I was being a Debbie Downer about this before," Courtney said.

"No apology needed," Dana said, firing up Big Red and driving back to Casa Verde.

"Slow... slow! Like you have coffee and muffins in here again," Courtney pleaded as she clutched the sidebar handle.

NINETEEN

The next morning, Dana was sitting on her favorite lounge chair on the veranda, reading a book and drinking coffee. Courtney was still asleep.

Ramón was already outside, working his machete on the yuca plants. A pile of yuca roots was stacked on the ground, making Dana crave garlic yuca fries. She made a mental note to herself to go fetch a few roots to fry up for later that night.

She was lost in thought with Wally coiled by her feet, sleeping. Despite Wally's snoring, she could hear the Pacific Ocean out in the distance. She took a sip of coffee. She was trying hard to not think about Barry Shy's body lying on the floor. And her mind wandered to her shuttered bookstore. *When will I be able to open for business?* she wondered.

The impromptu pop-up left her wanting to open her bookstore more than ever, so she itched to call Detective Picado for an update on the investigation. She looked at the time: 7:40 a.m. *I'll wait.*

At around eight a.m., a groggy Courtney stumbled out to the veranda with her own cup of coffee.

They exchanged good mornings, and Courtney plopped down on the sofa and yawned.

"How did you sleep?" Dana asked.

"Napoleon was putting on a show last night." Napoleon was the nickname of the howler monkey that seemed to love to make a ruckus right outside of Courtney's window. The howler monkey's howl is one of the loudest on the planet, and can be heard from miles away.

"Between the howler monkeys, tree frogs, and crickets, whoever thinks they'll enjoy the peace and quiet of the Costa Rican jungle at night is in for a surprise," Courtney said.

"Funny. I'm so used to the monkeys now that I hardly notice them raising Cain out there," Dana said.

"Not sure I could get used to that."

"Back in San Francisco, we got used to the sounds of wailing sirens, congested traffic, and the guy having a shouting match with himself. I'll take the jungle noise here over the concrete jungle any day of the week and twice on Sundays," Dana said, smiling.

"You really have adapted to living out here. And you were the poster child for city living."

Dana laughed. "Look around."

But it was true. She was a rare find in San Francisco, a native. She grew up living in the Western Addition district of the city, a stone's throw away from Alamo Square, which was overrun by herds of tourists looking for the Painted Ladies, expecting to see John Stamos and the Olsen twins roaming around the park like they did in Full House.

Dana never got the fascination with the Painted Ladies, a slew of multicolored Victorian and Edwardian houses. They were nice homes and all, but for the crowds they attracted, it was a bit bizarre. She'd take the natural beauty of the Guanacaste Province over a crowded park any day.

"I can't believe I've been here two days now, and you haven't asked me about him."

Dana knew who "him" was. Her ex-husband.

"Jeez, so yesterday you grilled me about Benny and now you're on to Phil."

"Don't get crabby with me, inquiring minds want to know."

"He's the last thing on my mind."

"You hear he's engaged?"

"Yep. It's all over Facebook."

"And you're okay with that?"

"That ship has long ago sailed away and is not coming back. What he does now with his life isn't my concern. I've moved on, and so has he. It's the magic of divorce."

"Fair enough. I'll shut up about men now."

"Thank you. I'm going to shower."

Dana was just stepping out of the shower when her phone trilled. It was a text message from Benny. He would be there in twenty minutes. They were going to have breakfast at the Qué Vista beach restaurant.

Dana quickly began to get ready and was done in ten minutes. She went downstairs, with Wally following her down the stairs.

A few minutes later, Courtney joined her.

"You got ready fast," Dana said since Courtney was slow as molasses when it came to getting ready to go anywhere.

"I'm starving," Courtney replied.

Dana's phone rang. It was Benny.

"What's up?"

"I seemed to have picked up a tail, so looks like you're going to have some company."

"Huh?"

"Picado is right behind me."

At first, Dana felt panic, then she felt relief.

"Good. I was planning on calling him anyway. I want to know when I can open my bookstore."

"Oh, brother," Courtney said.

Dana and Courtney were sitting on lawn chairs on the front porch of the house when they heard the buzzing of the front gate.

Ramón looked over at Dana.

"It's Benny," she said as she pressed on the remote control that opened the front gate.

She saw Benny's white Toyota Land Cruiser, and right behind him was Picado's white Toyota Hilux pickup truck. Its windows were tinted so dark that she couldn't tell who was driving until she was able to look through the windshield and saw Detective Rojas behind the wheel, as usual.

Both vehicles parked next to Dana's carport, and everyone seemed to get out of their respective vehicles at the same time.

Benny shrugged at Dana and looked over his shoulder at the detectives.

"Detectives, what can we do for you on this fine morning?" Benny said.

"You can ask your client to steer clear of my crime scene," Picado said as he made his way towards Dana aggressively. He glared at her and said, "Is that clear?"

"All I did was set up a small table in front of the locked gate of my bookstore, since it was supposed to be my grand opening and I was expecting people to show up. I wanted to be there to explain what's happening and why I'm not open yet. Officer Sanchez was there, and he said it was okay as long as I didn't go inside my bookstore or messed with the police tape you have all over my front door... which I didn't do. At all."

"Believe me, I already had word with Officer Sanchez about letting you stay. Now, I don't want you within twenty feet of my crime scene until I say it's okay. Am I being clear?"

"Yes, you are," Benny answered for Dana, since he could tell she was fuming with rage.

Courtney wrapped her arm around Dana's waist, trying to keep her calm.

Detective Gabriela Rojas stood with her arms crossed, looking down. Picado was her boss, so there was little she could do while Picado dressed Dana down.

Picado turned back towards his vehicle. Rojas snuck a sympathetic smile at Dana before turning to follow Picado back to the vehicle.

"Any idea as to when I can open my store?" Dana asked.

Benny closed his eyes.

Picado turned and yelled at her, "When my investigation is over, that's when."

They drove away as Dana, Courtney, and Benny stood there.

"I thought we agreed that even a pop-up wasn't such a good idea," Benny said, looking at Picado's truck's tail lights.

"You mentioned it. But I couldn't just not show up. I spent months promoting the grand-opening day, so I had to do something to let them know what's up and that I will be open for business as soon as that jerk gives me the okay."

Benny shook his head.

"Can he really do that? Don't you need a court order or something?" Courtney asked.

"Technically, you do, but it's not worth the fight. Let him blow off steam and let him be gone versus having to deal with court appointments and all that jazz," Benny said.

"I don't think I want to go to Qué Vista for breakfast," Dana said.

"Hey now, that man scares the living lights out of me, but I'm still hungry," Courtney said, holding her stomach.

"I can't handle running into the Gossip Brigade right now,"

Dana said, since the old ladies liked to hang out playing chess and canasta in the little park in front of the restaurant.

"Let's go somewhere else," Benny said, smiling. "You need a break from here."

They drove twenty minutes up to Nosara, the biggest smallest town that served as the canton seat for the Nosara District, which Mariposa Beach was part of.

Benny took them to his favorite restaurant in town, where they had a typical Costa Rican breakfast of eggs, gallo pinto, plátano maduro—savory fried plantains—corn tortillas, natilla cream, lots of fruits, and lots of coffee.

"So, do you think Picado is purposely keeping me closed because he doesn't like me?" Dana asked as they walked from the restaurant with their bellies full.

It was hot and humid—in other words, a typical day in the tropics. All three had their eyes out for the granizado man, an old man with a pushcart that sold ice cone confections that were delightful in the sweltering weather.

"Detective Picado has all the charm of a viper snake, but I don't think he would go that low as to prevent you from opening your store out of spite. Police investigations are slow. And because we're in a remote part of the country, things go even slower. It takes hours for the forensic team to drive down from San José or Liberia, and Picado himself is coming from Nicoya, which is two hours away. So things will move even slower than normal. It's just the way the cookie crumbles living down here in the tropics."

"I hope you're right. It just seems like he really does not like me."

"Oh, I'm sure he doesn't like you, but I don't think he would mess with you for sport," Benny said.

"Gee, thanks," Dana replied.

"Well, I love you, kid," Courtney said. "Hey, there he is, the ice cone man!"

The old man must have seen their excitement from a block away, because he smiled and waved at them as he pushed his cart in their direction.

They each had a cool granizado. Dana and Courtney chose the red cherry syrup and Benny the blue grape syrup. The old man topped off the ice cone by drizzling condensed milk and powdered milk over the syrup and handing the granizados over to his eager customers.

The three of them sat on a park bench, eating the granizados as the old man moved down the sidewalk, looking for more customers.

"It seems to me," Dana said, wiping her mouth clean from the ice treat, "that there is a long suspect list when it comes to who killed Barry Shy."

"He wasn't the most popular guy in town, that's for sure," Benny said.

"So this could take a long time to solve, especially if Picado is commuting from two hours away," Dana said.

"You think you can figure things out, don't you?" Courtney asked.

"No, but maybe I can help by just keeping my eyes and ears open. There is a murderer on the loose out there, after all."

"That's why Freddy has been in town every day," Benny said.

"But he's just hanging around the crime scene, AKA my darn bookstore."

"I see where you're going with this... solve this, and you can open your bookstore."

"Heavens to Betsy, what a great idea, Courtney."

Benny and Courtney both rolled their eyes and shook their heads.

"Detective Picado just told you to butt out. I think you should butt out," Benny said.

"You must not know her well enough yet. Anyone tells her she can't do something and she doubles down," Courtney said, grinning.

"I do, that's why I'm worried," Benny replied.

TWENTY

Dana and Benny weren't seeing eye to eye about trying to find out why Barry Shy was in her bookstore. Finding the answer to that mystery might solve the murder. But Benny saw it as just snooping, since he believed strongly that those were matters that should be left to the police.

She knew he had to be careful over his legal career, even though he insisted his concern was on her meddling into Detective Picado's investigation. She could be put away for preventive detention for interfering with police matters.

Courtney was downright terrified.

"We go for a drink at the Que Vista and ask the ladies of the Gossip Brigade some questions about what they might have heard or seen about Barry Shy's case, and that's it," Dana said.

"Why do you think that raucous group of canasta-playing old biddies would know anything worth knowing?" Courtney was not a fan of the Gossip Brigade. But the group of widows had grown on Dana. Yes, they were loud and brash and nosey, but the four longtime friends had thirty decades of living experience between them. The youngest of the group, Doña Chilla, was seventy-seven years old. Dana imagined you stopped caring about what people thought about you or holding back your tongue at that age. It was a liberating thought for Dana.

"It's a small town. A village, really, and those four ladies know everyone in a one-hundred-mile radius. They even knew Detective Picado when he was a child growing up in Liberia. So even that sourpuss shows reverence towards them, and I've seen him playing bridge with them. I doubt he does that as a sense of civic duty. He knows where to get information from, and they're a great source for information about the comings and goings around here."

Courtney shrugged. Benny added his own shrug, not being as convinced in the investigative powers of the Gossip Brigade.

The three of them walked into the Qué Vista restaurant ten minutes later.

The Gossip Brigade was already there, finishing their breakfast. Perfect timing, Dana thought, since they hadn't gotten into card mode.

The entire gang was there. The Gossip Brigade was made up of four old ladies that loved to play chess, canasta, and more than anything else, they loved to gossip and were shamelessly nosey, asking questions that would make the person on the receiving end of their queries blush.

Three of the old biddies had been friends since childhood. The newcomer joined the group in the 1960s.

They knew everyone in the province and loved to name-drop whenever they could. Their favorite topic was talking about that incorrigible little rascal back in the old neighborhood that so happened to have grown up to become the president of Costa Rica.

The way they talked about the president, they seemed to think he was still the same snot-nosed kid running around barefoot in the park.

"I didn't trust him back then, I don't trust him now," one would say as the others vehemently nodded in agreement.

If anyone had heard rumors or innuendos as to what happened to Barry Shy, it would be the Gossip Brigade.

Dana, Courtney, and Benny walked in single file. Dana smiled. She could hear the Gossip Brigade bickering all the way out in the parking lot.

"Sit anywhere you'd like," Jorge, the waiter, said to the group as they walked inside as he balanced two plates of eggs and gallo pinto and a plate of fruit.

"We're just here for your delicious Bloody Mary so we'll sit at the bar," Dana said as Jorge smiled and hurried away with the plates of food.

Dana looked over at the table of the Gossip Brigade who were digesting their breakfast as they prepared for what would be a boisterous game of canasta.

As the trio approached the group, Dana noticed they were cleaning up the table of all its free condiments packets and bread rolls, which they shoved into their oversized purses. Dana couldn't help but smile. They lived without shame or filters, and she actually admired that.

"Hello, ladies," Dana said.

The ladies all turned to look up at Dana with eyes squinting, faces scrunched up, working hard to get their vision into focus. "Oh, hello Dana," Doña Marta said.

"Who's your pretty friend?" asked Doña Amada, the short and pudgy leader of the brigade.

Dana opened her mouth to respond, but Doña Chilla interrupted her. "That's Dana's friend from San Francisco. She was down here a few months ago." Dana was impressed with her memory. "Your name is Courtney, right, dear?"

"That's right," Courtney said, smiling.

Dana hoped her memory was that sharp when she was in her late seventies.

"You have an amazing memory," Dana said to Doña Chilla with a grin. "Courtney stayed with me when I first moved down here, but she went back home to San Francisco a few months ago and now she's back for another visit."

"How are you holding up, dear? You are going through a lot of awful things since moving to town," Doña Marta said.

And we're off and running, Dana thought.

"Oh, I'm fine. Thanks for asking. But I am a bit anxious, since I was supposed to have opened my bookstore already but the police won't let me."

"That Juan Picado has always been insufferable," Doña Amada said as she removed a deck of cards from her purse.

"Ever since we was a little boy he's been a handful," Doña Marta added.

"Can't say I disagree. He has me shut me down, indefinitely."

"That Picado, always walking around like he has a pebble in his shoe. He thinks he's Tarzan's mother and he isn't even Cheetah's mom," said Doña Luz, the comedian of the group, as the rest of the brigade broke out in a boisterous chorus of laughter.

Dana joined them in laughter. Benny and Courtney stood there with thin grins on their faces.

"You're terrible," Doña Chilla said. Although she was the youngest one of the group, her hands and face had enough wrinkles to give a Shar-Pei a run for its money. Dana figured a lifetime spent at the family coffee farm under the blazing tropical sun was the likely culprit.

She was the sweet one of the group. A bit on the shy side in comparison to the rest of the brigade.

Time to start pumping the well for information, Dana

thought. "So, what have you ladies heard through the grapevine?"

"Why do you think we would know anything about that?" Doña Marta said, sounding insulted. All that was missing was for her to clutch at her pearls.

"Oh, stop your babe in the woods routine, Marta, you're the biggest gossip of the group," Doña Amada barked. She had a low, wheezing sound to her voice after sixty years puffing on cigarettes.

Dana, Benny, and Courtney stood there for a few seconds in awkward silence. "I just pay attention to things, that's all," Doña Marta replied, focusing her attention on the deck of cards on the table.

"And you get all the best dirt in the village," Doña Luz said, laughing so hard she started to cough.

"Are you all right, Doña Luz?" Benny asked.

"She needs mouth-to-mouth resuscitation from you," Doña Amada said, cackling.

Benny turned beet red. Dana blushed too, and she looked over at Courtney, who mouthed *Wow* to her.

"Amada, you are so crude," Doña Luz snapped angrily.

Dana was relieved when the waiter interrupted and began bussing the table. As soon as he was gone with the stack of dirty dishes, Doña Amada began to set up for their card game.

"Any idea why Barry Shy would have broken into my bookstore?" Dana said, trying to steer the conversation back towards something that might shed more light about what happened.

"Oh, he was a weirdo," Doña Amada said.

"Nothing he did would surprise me," Doña Luz added.

"They'll probably find dead bodies buried out in his land," Doña Marta added.

"You shouldn't speak ill of the dead," Doña Chilla said, giving herself the sign of the cross.

Dana was having a hard time keeping up.

"Come on, Marta, tell them what you told us yesterday so we can get this game started, " Doña Amada said, sounding annoyed at Dana's snooping and giving her a sideways glance before turning her full attention back to setting up for the game.

"Well..." Doña Marta said, looking around as if to make sure no one was eavesdropping. She crooked her arthritically misshapen index finger to beckon Dana to come closer, which she did.

Doña Marta said, in almost a whisper, "I overheard that pretty policewoman talking on her phone outside of Mindy's coffee shop, and she was asking whomever she was talking to for information on Ike, since there was some sort of feud between those two."

"Ike Van de Berg?" Dana asked incredulously.

"That's the only Ike around here," Doña Amada butted in.

Ike Van de Berg was a Dutchman who had moved to Costa Rica in the seventies and came to Mariposa Beach in the eighties to open his restaurant. The Oceanview Restaurant was about a ten-minute drive up the mountain from Mariposa Beach. The restaurant was perched on the headland above the cliffs overlooking the Pacific Ocean. The restaurant was built in a European neo-classical style not commonly seen in Costa Rica, but Ike had explained to Dana that he wanted his restaurant to have the look and feel of ancient Greek architecture.

Dana had learned that he had even named his restaurant Mount Olympus, but after a year he changed it to the more descriptive and marketable Oceanview.

It was the only fine dining restaurant in a fifteen-mile radius from Mariposa Beach where the waiters wore thin black neckties. Ike used to prohibit the use of T-shirts and shorts from his guests, but having a restaurant in midst of beach country, he relented a few years ago, although Dana would imagine eating there in shorts would make you feel out of place.

She and Courtney had dinner there once when she first moved down to Mariposa Beach. The restaurant's architecture and views were stunning. The service was top-notch. But the food was a bit bland and boring. Ike seemed like an intense man, and he had a reputation for being tough on his restaurant staff, but he was nice to her.

He was a big man with a shaved head. He was in his late sixties. His English and Spanish were excellent, but he couldn't lose his Dutch accent even after living for decades in Costa Rica.

She could see him losing his top in a road-rage type deal, but she couldn't imagine he would have killed anyone, Barry Shy included.

Dana, Benny, and Courtney were still standing there when Doña Amada was done setting up for their game of canasta, so she shooed them away with a wave of the hand. "Game time, no more gossip," she said dismissively, so Dana, Benny, and Courtney made their way to the bar for their Bloody Marys.

The bar was on the other end of the restaurant from where the Gossip Brigade were sitting so they could discuss what they had just learned without having to worry about the ladies eavesdropping, although the group seemed so enthralled with their card game that they probably didn't care what they were talking about for once.

Jorge was doing double-duty as a waiter and bartender.

"You're doing it all this morning, Jorge," Dana said with a smile.

"The bartender doesn't come until the afternoon," Jorge said making Dana feel like a lush although she knew he didn't mean anything by it.

"Three Bloody Marys, extra green olives for me, please," Dana said.

"And coffee, please," Courtney added as Jorge began to turn away to make the drinks.

"Coming right up," he said.

As Jorge prepared the drinks another waiter brought over a black thermal coffee carafe along with three cups, much to the delight of Courtney.

"I need, I need, I need," she said jokingly as she picked up the carafe and poured herself a cup.

"I can't imagine Ike Van de Berg would be involved with murder," Dana said.

"Who is he?" Courtney asked sipping coffee.

"You met him once when we went to his Oceanview Restaurant," Dana explained.

"Oh, yeah, stocky bald Dutch guy, right?" Courtney asked.

"That's him."

"He's going for that Daddy Warbucks look," Courtney said.

Dana and Benny laughed at Courtney's comparison, which wasn't too far off.

"He's been living in Costa Rica for over forty years," Benny said. "And I agree, I can't imagine he would get mixed up in something like murder."

"Sounds like they had a feud, though," Courtney said.

Benny laughed. "If having a feud with Barry Shy makes you a prime suspect, then everyone in Mariposa Beach is a suspect, Dana and myself included."

"I'm assuming the pretty policewoman Doña Marta mentioned was Gabriela Rojas," Dana said. Benny agreed. *So you think she's pretty*, Dana thought, feeling a twinge of jealousy. *Whoa, don't go there.*

"Maybe there is more to their feud than meets the eye," Dana said.

Jorge interrupted their brainstorming session with their Bloody Mary drinks.

"We might as well go talk to Ike," Dana said.

"No way, he might be a murderer and you're going to let him know we know that or are thinking that? We'll be next on the chopping block," Courtney said grabbing a celery stick from her Bloody Mary and snapping it in half for dramatic effect.

"I don't think for a New York minute that Ike killed Barry," Benny said.

"Besides, if we heard about it from the Gossip Brigade, that means just about everyone in town has heard it too, including Ike," Dana said.

"Okay, but still, it's not wise to kick a hornets' nest—two hornets' nests, actually: a possible killer, and Detective Picado if he finds outs we went out there to question one of his possible suspects."

Dana shrugged.

"Preventive detention," Courtney said, her voice shaky pointing at Dana with the celery stick. "Three months in jail without having to charge us with anything."

"Well. Maybe I'll just run into him. Start up a conversation about Barry Shy and my bookstore. See what Ike has to say," Dana said.

Benny and Courtney exchanged worried glances.

"CANASTA!" one of the old ladies from the Gossip Brigade shouted as they heard Doña Amada protest the results and accuse Doña Luz of cheating.

TWENTY-ONE

"Hey, hon, the usual?" Mindy asked Dana as soon as she set foot inside the coffee shop before the door even closed behind her.

There was an attractive young couple decked out in swimwear and flip-flops, waiting for their order. They both turned as if to see who was the regular that had just walked in a la Norm Peterson in *Cheers*. The handsome couple smiled, and Dana blushed.

"I guess I'm getting way too boring and predictable."

Mindy laughed. "An everything bagel with mango cream cheese and large latte, coming right up."

Mindy disappeared to the back to work on the orders as Dana chatted with the young couple for about a minute.

They were boyfriend and girlfriend from Australia, which made Dana wonder why they would travel halfway across the globe to the Guanacaste Province when they had the Gold Coast in their backyard.

Costa Rica was a beautiful country with breathtaking beaches, and its proximity to the US was a nice perk. *But*, she thought, *I don't think I would fly over eight thousand miles over the Pacific Ocean to get here if I had the Great Barrier Reef in my home turf. Grass is greener,* she figured.

Dana learned that the young couple was actually staying down by Samara, which was about a twenty-minute drive down the coast, but they had heard great things about Mindy's food, so they drove up in their rental car to check it out.

Mindy re-emerged from the kitchen with the couple's order.

They said their goodbyes as they left with half a dozen of Mindy's soft and moist bagels—a mix of sesame and onion bagels—and a pint of her strawberry cream cheese.

Tourists from within a twenty-mile radius would make the trek to Mindy's Coffee and Bagels. And in the mornings, the lines sometimes snaked out the door.

Big Mike had joked the other day that Mindy's place was beating out the calm, bright-blue water and white-sand beach as the main tourist draw to Mariposa Beach.

Dana felt a little jealous. No one would make that long of a haul for a used book. Moot point anyway, since her bookstore remained a crime scene.

Big Mike was keen on saying that Mindy got tourists to town, and once they were full and happy, they perused other stores in town.

"Cute couple," Mindy said to Dana as she watched them go out to the parking lot and get into a Suzuki convertible.

"They have never been to Mariposa Beach. They're staying in the more popular surfer beach town, but they drove up here just for your bagels and cream cheese. Big Mike was right, you're like our main tourist attraction," Dana said, smiling.

Mindy laughed, then added, "Well, I'm not so sure about that. I saw them in town a couple days ago."

"Are you sure? They said they had never been here before."

"He looks like Channing Tatum and she looks like Gisele

Bündchen. Hard to mistake them, so yes, I'm sure it was them," Mindy said, laughing.

Dana looked out the window. There was a cloud of dust and dirt left behind as they drove away.

"Oh, honey, you have that Columbo look to you. It's no big deal, all the beach communities up and down the coast look pretty much the same, so I'm sure they just forgot. It's quite common with the off the beaten path beach town hopping tourists," Mindy explained.

"They came for your bagels and cream cheese, so I would think they would remember that," Dana said.

"Well, I think there is another tourist you should be more worried about," Mindy said.

"Really, who?" Dana's eyebrows arched as she put her elbows on the counter and leaned forward to get closer to Mindy.

"Your book-loving loudmouth."

Dana knew she meant Chris Smith from Chicago.

"So what did he want?"

"He was like Mr. Twenty Questions about you. Made me very uncomfortable."

"What kind of questions?"

"About your bookstore. When was it going to open. If you come here a lot. And if you lived near here. He tried to disguise the questions as harmless chitchat, but he was getting way too personal and specific about things."

"Example?"

"Well," Mindy stopped to think for a moment, "he didn't come out and ask me where you lived, but he said it must be nice for you to live so close to the bookstore, like he was fishing, so I lied and told him I don't know where you live. When I asked him why he wanted to know that, he got all sheepish and muttered he was curious, and then he hightailed it out of here. It was weird. Creepy."

"He has been hanging around for days now trying to get into my bookstore. At first it was just annoying because he's so pushy and rude, but now, you're right, it's darn creepy."

"You think he's like obsessed with you and is like one of those stalkers?"

"I don't know about that. He seems to be obsessed with my books, not me."

Dana saw by Mindy's reaction that the same idea had just dinged in her head too.

"Obsessed enough to break into my bookstore, since I wouldn't let him in."

Mindy nodded and wrapped her arms around her body, feeling a chill down her spine, and it wasn't because of the air conditioner blasting away.

"You need to report him to the police," Mindy said.

Dana nodded in agreement.

Dana thanked Mindy for having her back and made her way down to the beach, where Courtney was waiting for her.

Courtney had set up a nice spot underneath a fallen palm that offered a nice shade. She had set up the two portable lawn chairs she had brought along and a large beach towel next to the chair, where she had put her bags and a big jug of ice water that prevented the towel from being stolen by the wind.

"Hey, you," Dana said as she sat down on the empty chair next to Courtney, "nice spot."

"Yeah, this is perfect for the long haul."

After everything that had been going on, they decided to just chill for a couple hours on the beach.

"You were gone awhile. Mindy's was busy?"

"Not really, but I talked with her for a bit. Get this..."

Dana told Courtney what Mindy had shared about the loudmouth and the Australian couple that seemed to have lied about having been to Mariposa Beach before.

Courtney didn't seem too worried about the Australians, but she turned ashen when Dana told her all about the loudmouth asking Mindy about her and trying to fish the location of her home out of her.

"You're right, creepy as heck," Courtney said.

Dana nodded in agreement.

"It seems he has been eager to get into my bookstore since day one, and lo and behold, my bookstore is broken into and Barry winds up dead."

"So you think he was in cahoots with Barry Shy to break into your store?"

"I don't know what to think about those two, but it seems too much of a coincidence. It's something we need to follow up on."

"Excuse me? We? You mean it's something for the police to follow up with."

"I guess you're right. But I don't even think they're in town right now."

"Don't care. Call them. I'm sure they'll come down," Courtney said, sounding worried.

Dana mulled it over.

"Dana?"

"What? I'll call the police, but I can check up on a couple of things to figure out what's up with Chris Smith from Chicago."

Courtney looked at her with an exasperated expression. "That Picado guy will hit the roof if he finds out that this guy has been acting suspicious about your bookstore and you didn't tell him and you started to snoop around him," Courtney warned.

"Maybe he has nothing to do with anything and he's just one of those annoying types of people that roam the earth in spades. They do exist, you know. So I don't want to jam up anyone with the likes of Picado for no reason."

"To be honest, girl, that's the police's job to figure out if something is important or not."

Dana shrugged. She knew Courtney was right, but that wasn't going to stop her from looking a bit closer into the loud-mouth to see if he had anything to do with the break-in and murder in her bookstore.

Courtney crossed her arms and sighed. "That shrug you just gave me and your silence speak loudly, you know that, right?"

Dana smiled. "You know me so well."

Courtney sighed even louder. "Pass me a bagel."

"Tell you what," Dana said, passing her the bagel, "I call Detective Rojas and let her know. That way they can look into it and I don't have to deal with Picado."

"That's all I ask that you get the police involved," Courtney said, unwrapping the bagel and spreading mango cream cheese on it.

"After I call her, we can check on a couple things."

"I thought we were just hanging out at the beach."

"Hello," Dana said, waving her hands in the air, "we're hanging out at the beach."

"May you get sand in your bagel," Courtney said, taking a bite of her own bagel as Dana laughed.

"Meany."

TWENTY-TWO

After an hour at the beach, Dana and Courtney headed back to Casa Verde, where they plopped on the lounge chairs in the veranda.

Courtney was on her laptop, checking up on work emails. Dana had her notebook laid out in front of her and was writing her thoughts out about Ike, Barry Shy, the Australian couple, and her loudmouth. As she wrote, Wally decided he wanted attention, so he began purring and rubbing up against her, and every time she tried to write on her notebook, Wally would bat at the pen with his right paw like it was a butterfly.

After a minute or two of this, an exasperated Dana would plead for Wally to stop and be a good kitty. He would give her a sideway glance as if to say *How dare you speak to me in that tone,* and as soon as she put the pen to paper, Wally was on it like white on rice.

Courtney laughed. "I told you that cat was trouble the day he waltzed in here like he owned the place."

"I know how to distract him," Dana said. She got up and Wally plopped on Dana's notebook and stretched out on it. He looked at her as if to say *To the victor go the spoils.*

Dana went downstairs to the kitchen. She had a plastic container of Wally's favorite food: a can of Sardimar tuna Dana mixed with leftover rice and ground beef. As soon as she pried the plastic lid off and it made that telltale sound, she heard Wally running downstairs like the veranda was on fire. She could hear Courtney laughing and yelling, "Go, kitty, go!"

"Here you go," Dana said, putting down his dish. Wally began to stuff his face, having forgotten about her notebook and pen.

Dana went back upstairs and smiled proudly at Courtney.

"No fuss, no muss," she said, wiping her hands together.

"That will teach him. Be a pain, get food," Courtney said facetiously.

Dana rolled her eyes and shrugged her shoulders. She knew she was a softy when it came to animals—nothing new there.

"Okay," Dana said, plopping back down on her chair, "where was I?"

"On your way to preventive detention," Courtney said.

Dana ignored her.

"I need to find out why the police are looking at Ike. It can't be just because Barry and Ike didn't get along or because they had a dispute. Barry had disputes with everyone in town, myself included. So why do they like Ike?"

Courtney chuckled. "I get it, *I like Ike,*" Dana said, referring to the slogan used during Dwight David "Ike" Eisenhower's presidential campaigns in the fifties.

Dana refocused on the notebook. "So what happened between them to spike the police's interest in Ike?" Dana said. Although she said it out loud, she was mostly speaking to herself. Courtney knew as much, so she continued to tap away on her laptop, letting Dana do her thing.

"We also have my loudmouth, who has been a royal pain about wanting to see my books. So, my first question is, why? He gave me a cockamamie story about being a book lover and collector, but why would he think I would have anything of value when I told him over and over I would be selling used paperback beach reads?"

"Maybe he's watched too much of *American Pickers* on the History Channel and thinks you're unknowingly sitting on a treasure trove of books that he can buy for a buck and sell for a million bucks," Courtney said, looking up from her laptop.

"There is no way..." Dana said, trailing off, lost in thought.

"No way what?"

"I can't believe I forgot to tell you, but I was so busy with the store opening, and I didn't know you were coming, but Benny and I did find a treasure trove of very valuable books hidden inside a secret compartment built into the floor of my den."

"Books? How valuable could they be?"

"You'd be amazed, but first-edition books are very valuable and sought after, and Uncle Blake had a lot of them in his collection."

"How valuable?"

"I really don't know yet. But one of the books alone could be worth ten grand."

"What?" Courtney said, almost falling from the chair.

"I told you, very valuable. But it's not verified, so it could be worth nothing more than a dollar. I've been doing some preliminary research, talking with a book expert in New York. But we're far from putting a definitive value to the collection."

"Are those books in the bookstore?"

"Oh, no way. I have those books separate. Benny actually took them up to the city, where he put them in a climate-controlled storage unit until we can sit down and figure out their worth. But there is no way that Chris Smith could know about them."

"It's probably just a coincidence then and he just thinks you might have something of value from a collector's perspective, which explains why he wants first crack at perusing your inventory," Courtney said.

"Yes, that makes more sense. How could he know? Only I, Benny, and now you know about those books."

"What about the book expert in New York?"

"Greyson?" Dana sounded surprised.

"Well, I don't know his name, but you said you were talking with a book expert in New York. So he knows, right?"

"Yes, Greyson Bay, but he's never even been to Costa Rica. And he's standing to make a nice commission if I decide to sell these books, so the last thing he would want is the loudmouth to get his hands on those books."

"Okay, and how does Barry Shy fit into all this?"

"That's the big mystery, isn't it? I can't see him knowing or caring about first-edition books."

"Maybe he and Chris Smith teamed up, thinking your pricey books were at the bookstore."

"I can't imagine Barry Shy knew the loudmouth, or that he would be in cahoots to rob me of my books. The man lived off the land in a shack without electricity or running water. He couldn't care less about money."

Dana was silent for a moment, thinking it over in her head.

"I can just ask the loudmouth if he knew Barry or if he had heard about my first editions."

"No way, Dana. Don't tell me you want to confront the loudmouth and ask him that."

"No."

"Good," a relieved Courtney replied.

"That might freak him out. I don't want to spook him so he runs back to Chicago. I think we need to run into him. By accident." Dana added air quotes when she said *accident*.

"I meant good as in you're not even going to get near this

man. I mean, really, you want to run into a possible murderer and start asking him questions about a burglary and murder he might be behind?"

"Well, only in broad daylight with people around. Sure, why not?"

"Why not? Um, death, harm, preventive detention, should I go on?" Courtney said.

She sounded angry, which Dana understood. She was worried about what she might get them into, so she decided not to bounce this stuff off her anymore. But Dana was certain about one thing: it seemed that Chris Smith was always hanging around near the bookstore.

TWENTY-THREE

Dana and Courtney jumped into Big Red to head back to Mindy's cafe. Courtney was not happy about it at all, but Dana figured if she wanted to run into the loudmouth, it would be near Ark Row and Mindy's place.

Besides, she wanted to ask some questions about the loudmouth to Mindy.

"Hey ladies," Mindy greeted the two warmly as they made their way inside.

They exchanged pleasantries, Dana waved at Mindy's husband, Leo, who peeked out from the kitchen, and then they chitchatted for a moment.

Dana ordered another latte. Courtney ordered an iced café mocha.

"Cold coffee, yuck," Dana said, grinning.

"It feels like we're on the surface of the sun out there," Courtney said defensively.

"What can I say, I always like my coffee senior citizen hot."

All three of them shared a laugh.

While they waited for their coffee, Dana got into it.

"Mindy, I was wondering about my loudmouth stalker."

Mindy visibly tensed up.

"What about him?"

"Have you seen him around town today?"

"No it's been a quiet day. Are you worried about running into him?"

Courtney guffawed at the question. "She *wants* to run into him," Courtney said.

Mindy looked confused as Dana gave Courtney a shush look.

"Oh, honey, you're not planning on confronting him, are you?" Mindy asked sounding worried.

"I'm just trying to figure out why he's so darn interested in my bookstore."

"He told you he's a book collector," Courtney said.

"Who just happened to be in town after I found my uncle's valuable book collection."

"Stranger things have happened," Courtney said.

"You think he broke into your bookstore?" Mindy asked, sounding as if it had just dawned on her.

"Timing seems to work."

"But then that means he was working with Barry Shy, so then that would mean... he killed Barry?"

"I have no idea."

Leo came from out of the back kitchen. "You need to call the police if you have any type of suspicion about this guy. Do not try to find him yourself or talk to him. For Pete's sake, this guy could be very dangerous."

"I agree with Leo, Dana. Let the police deal with this," Mindy said.

"Thank you," Courtney said, sounding relieved she wasn't the only one thinking rationally.

Dana thanked Mindy and Leo for the coffees and their help and advice.

Once outside, Dana and Courtney climbed back into Big Red.

Dana sat there quietly for a moment, both hands on the steering wheel.

"You want to go up there to the resort to find this Chris Smith, don't you?"

Dana smiled. "Yep." She fired up Big Red and took off towards the Tranquil Bay Resort.

It was about a ten-minute drive up to the luxurious jungle-resort.

The resort was the pride and joy of Gustavo Barca, a Venezuelan multimillionaire that was part of the great Venezuela exodus that had migrated to Costa Rica after years of political and economic unrest there.

Dana had loathed Barca since he wanted to buy Casa Verde to tear it down and make her land part of his private posh resort. He had bankrolled her cousin's legal fees when he contested her uncle's will.

Barca lost and slithered away in retreat—not that he gave up on his dream of unleashing bulldozers on Casa Verde, though. And he would always have a smug look on his face when she ran into him around the coast, and he always would do the same thing when he saw her: he would grin and rub his thumb and index finger together, giving her the international money gesture, and would follow that with the "call me" finger gesture.

Dana wanted to respond with the one-finger gesture that was also well known internationally, but she always took the high road and would just say nope.

So she avoided the resort like there was an outbreak of bubonic plague within its protective walls and posh interiors.

"Ugh, I hate coming here," Dana said as she drove up to the front gate.

"Good, make a U-turn and let's get out of here," Courtney pleaded.

The uniformed security guard looked at the two of them and he raised the front gate security arm and waved them through.

"Nothing is going to happen in here with all the people staying here and the staff and security guards, don't worry," Dana said as she drove up to the front lobby area.

"Welcome, Doña Dana," the red-shirted valet said, looking at Big Red.

"Hello," Dana said, handing him the keys. She didn't remember his name—it was only her third trip up the mountain to the resort—but she did recall how much the valet loved Big Red.

"I see you're taking very good care of her," he said, ogling the car.

Dana glanced at his nametag. "I try my best, Frank."

Once inside, Claudio Villalobos, the concierge manager for the resort, greeted her warmly. He was the son of Casa Verde's caretakers, Ramón and Carmen Villalobos.

Claudio had helped Dana before, so she had texted him about coming up to the resort.

It was a risky move for the young man who dreamed of one day opening his own hotel right in Mariposa Beach, since he worked for Gustavo Barca and he would have been fired on the spot if he found out that he had provided information to Dana during her legal battle for Casa Verde.

Claudio loved Dana's uncle, who had paid for his college education in hotel management, and he wasn't too keen on letting Barca take over Casa Verde, since he didn't hide the fact that his plans for the property meant tossing his parents out of their home too.

To her relief, Barca wasn't around anyway.

"We could have met at your parents' house, Claudio. I get nervous that you'll get in trouble being seen with me here at the resort," Dana said, looking around like she was casing the joint.

"Mr. Barca is on a shopping trip at Miami with his wife. He won't be back until next week, so I'm not worried. Besides," he said, unable to suppress a wide smile, he leaned in close to Dana, "my days here are numbered. I've been offered a position at the Four Seasons in the Papagayo Peninsula."

"Wow, congrats," Dana said, hugging him. Courtney also offered her congratulations. "When do you start there?"

"I'm giving them my two weeks' notice on Monday, so please keep this just between us."

"Of course, you got it. So, how do your parents feel about you leaving town?"

The Four Seasons resort was a three-hour car ride away from Mariposa Beach on the other side of the Guanacaste province.

"It's a better job. Assistant to the General Manager. A big pay bump, so they're happy for me, and they're also glad that I'm getting away from *you know who and his mini me*," he said, whispering. Dana knew he was referring to Gustavo Barca and his insufferable general manager for the resort—a micro-manager whose lips seemed to be surgically attached to Barca's behind.

Dana giggled. "I'm happy for you, but I'm going to miss you."

"I'll be coming around a lot to visit my parents, so you won't be getting rid of me that easily."

"Good," Dana said. "So... did you find anything about Chris Smith?"

"I was just going to text you back so you could save the drive up. I'm afraid he's not staying here," Claudio said.

"Did he check out?"

"No, he never checked in. I went back two months, and there hasn't been a Chris Smith from Chicago checked in at all."

Dana was surprised.

"Chris Smith is a common name. Any other people with that name from some other state?" Dana asked.

"There were a few Smiths but we haven't had any guests named Chris Smith in the last couple months."

"Well, that puts a damper on things," Dana replied.

"You drove all the way up here, why not stay for lunch? On the house," Claudio said, offering two free lunch vouchers.

As much as Dana loathed Gustavo Barca and what he wanted to do to her home, she couldn't deny that the man went all out with his resort, including its restaurants.

"Why not?" Dana said.

"Yay, I'm starving, and the food here is so good," Courtney said, taking the vouchers from Claudio before Dana could change her mind.

"Thank you so much, Claudio."

TWENTY-FOUR

After striking out on finding Chris Smith or whatever his real name was at the resort, Dana and Courtney headed back to Casa Verde, but at least their bellies were full with a delicious gourmet meal that was on Barca's dime. It made the meal that much more scrumptious for Dana.

"He probably gave Mindy a fake name and lied about where he was staying, which really raises my suspicions about him," Dana said as she slowed down to avoid a huge pothole in the middle of the road.

They made it back to Casa Verde and settled in.

"What now?" Courtney asked as she plopped down on the living room sofa.

Just then Dana's phone buzzed. Dana looked down at a text message from Mindy.

"Holy cow!"

"What?"

"Chris Smith was at Mindy's cafe just now."

"Don't tell me you want to rush down there."

"No. Mindy just sent me his picture."

Courtney sprang from the couch towards Dana. "Let me

see," she said, peering into the phone's screen. Dana was looking at the man that had been so pushy and rude to her for the better part of a week.

"Hmmm," Courtney said.

"What?"

"I was expecting a muscled-up thug, but he looks like Dwight Schrute."

"And he's just as annoying as Dwight Schrute."

"So what now?"

"I have his picture. If anyone can help me put a name to the face, it's Bucky," Dana said, referring to her friend in Silicon Valley, Bucky Moreland, who had designed her bookselling software.

Dana called Bucky right away and they connected via FaceTime.

He was more than happy to help out. He loved technical challenges, and figuring out who the loudmouth really was from a single, somewhat blurry iPhone photograph was right up his alley.

"Ooh, so NSA-like. I'm *In Like Flint*," he had told Dana.

After hanging up with Bucky, Dana joined Courtney in the kitchen, where she was in the process of making a pitcher of banana daiquiri. "Bucky is off and running," she informed her.

Courtney looked up from the center island, where she had all the accoutrements needed for her banana daiquiri: Flor de Caña rum from Nicaragua, a can of coconut milk, lime juice—courtesy of the lime tree in the backyard—sugar, ice, and bananas—also courtesy from the banana plants in the backyard.

Courtney gave her a thin smile as she sliced the limes. Dana knew she didn't approve of her snooping.

"He said to give him a couple of days. I hope it doesn't take him that long to find out who this guy is."

"So now you're into facial-recognition snooping," Courtney said without looking up from her chopping.

"Maybe Bucky can dig up something we can pass along to the police so everyone is happy," Dana said.

"Maybe the police will solve this before Bucky and you will still get in trouble for meddling with a police investigation," was Courtney's brusque reply.

"Hey, no complaints from me if Detective Picado can solve this and I can open my bookstore."

"He'll probably give you the go-ahead to open your store pretty soon. They don't need to keep it closed once all the forensic stuff is done, even if they haven't caught the killer."

Courtney looked down at her handiwork. Everything was ready, so she tossed all the goodies into the blender. Before Dana could reply, the blender roared to life.

She poured the drinks into two tall glasses, which she then garnered with a thin wedge of lime.

"Beautiful. You haven't lost your touch," Dana said, referring to Courtney's days as a bartender.

Unlike a lot of the Berkeley students, Dana and Courtney didn't come from money, so they were able to attend thanks to in-state tuition pricing, academic scholarships, swim team scholarship, and working as servers and bartenders in restaurants and bars around the Bay Area.

They sat out on the deck, watching the sunset and sipping on their drinks.

"It really is beautiful here. So nice and quiet compared to San Francisco. I'm not used to hearing crickets and critters at night, just sirens and people acting stupid," Courtney said.

"You can see why I like it here despite the craziness I've had to deal with since moving down here."

"It's ironic. You moved down here for peace and quiet."

It was an irony that hadn't been lost on Dana.

"Mmm, it's good," she said, tasting the tropical drink.

"So what's up with Benny?" Courtney asked.

"He's been working up in San José, but he's making his way back for the weekend."

"That's not what I meant." Courtney took a sip of her drink, eyeing her mischievously. "I mean what's going on between you two?"

"I've already told you: nothing, strictly friends with a side of legal help when I need it."

"Well, the chemistry between you two is off the charts."

Dana did an actual eye roll.

"It's true!"

"The chemistry was off the charts with Phil too... look how that ended," Dana was referring to Phil Miller, her ex-husband.

"Slow down, girlfriend. I'm not saying you should marry the guy, just date him."

Dana rolled her eyes again. She couldn't help it.

"Don't roll your eyes at me, missy," Courtney said, head to one side, her hands on her hips.

The two friends laughed.

"But seriously... it's obvious like that nose on your face that Benny is into you and you're into him, and I'm not talking about being pals."

Dana blushed. She couldn't throw a fast one by her.

Just then her phone buzzed, so she glanced down. As if he knew they were talking about him, it was from Benny, letting her know that he was a couple hours away from Mariposa Beach. He told her he would drive straight to her place, then the three of them could go out to dinner.

"So, we have a couple hours before Benny gets here," Dana said.

"What do you want to do?"

Sleep had been hard to come by the last few days, but after a couple daiquiris, she felt a bit sleepy, so Dana opted for a nap.

"Do you mind if I take a nap?"

"No, not at all. Go get some sleep. I have some work to do, so I'll jump on my laptop."

Dana slept for a couple hours with Wally curled up next to her. She sat up in bed and checked on the time.

"Whoa, Wally, any more sleep and this wouldn't have been a nap, but just out-cold sleeping."

She showered and dressed and joined Courtney downstairs, chitchatting until Benny arrived on time, as usual.

The three of them caught up for a while out on the deck.

He was giving the latest updates from San José and Dana updating him on her and Bucky's "investigation," as she called it.

"You mean snooping," Benny said.

"Are you two sharing notes? All you need is for you to get my mom into the disapproval tango you guys are doing."

"Don't tempt me," Courtney said, smiling.

"I just wish you would let the police do their job," Benny said seriously.

"Ditto," Courtney added.

"I am, but let's see what Bucky comes up with. I want to know who this Chris Smith is anyway, since he's been stalking me for days. It's not like the police would do anything about that, and I don't want to pull police resources from finding Barry's killer so I can open my bookstore. So as far as I can tell, it can't hurt to let Bucky work his tech magic."

Benny and Courtney exchanged a nervous glance.

"Anyway. I don't want to talk about this anymore. I'm starving. Let's go get dinner."

They decided to go someplace different for dinner this time, not their usual eating haunts of Mariposa Beach, which boiled down to the Qué Vista Restaurant or Linda's Soda.

"Let's go for a gourmet meal at the Oceanview Restaurant?" Dana suggested.

"The Dutchman's place?" Courtney asked, sounding suspicious.

"Yeah, Ike's place."

Benny and Courtney gave her an incredulous look at the same time.

"What?"

"Last time we ate there, you weren't very impressed with the food," Courtney said.

"Ah, but now that Ike is on the radar of Picado's investigation..." Benny added.

TWENTY-FIVE

"Dana, am I glad to see you, welcome," Ike Van de Berg greeted Dana, Benny, and Courtney at the door of his restaurant. The greeting confused Dana. She had chatted with Ike a few times since she moved to Mariposa Beach, and this was only her second visit to his restaurant, so it's not like they were on super friendly terms.

"Glad... to... see you, too..." Dana replied confused, realizing she said it in a tone that sounded more like a question.

Ike sat them at one of the best tables in the restaurant, next to the window overlooking the ocean. The restaurant was built on the edge of a steep cliff, so the table gave the appearance of teetering on the edge of the cliff.

Eduardo, the sommelier, greeted them as they settled in. Based on his expert recommendations, they picked a French red wine.

"This is nice," Benny said, sounding surprised. Dana smiled. She knew both of her friends were upset about coming to Ike's restaurant, since they weren't there for the dinner or the ambience but to snoop.

"That was a warm greeting you got from Ike," Courtney said.

"Right?" Dana replied, sounding relieved she wasn't the only one that picked up on that vibe.

Before they could talk about it further, Eduardo was back with the wine; he took his sommelier duties seriously, showing the bottle to the table, seeking approval before uncorking it. Dana smiled and nodded, and he proceeded to open the bottle and pour a tasting sample into Dana's glass. She didn't recall being the one that ordered it, but since she had been given the responsibility to vet the wine, she picked up the glass and brought it to her nose sniffing a couple times, then took a small sip.

"Delicious, thank you."

"The bottle is complimentary from Don Ike," Eduardo said as he poured.

"Okay, wow, thanks," Dana said as Eduardo filled Courtney and Benny's glasses.

"Enjoy," he said walking away.

"What's up with that?" Courtney asked.

"I don't have a clue," Dana said.

"Ike's closefisted about how many bread rolls he serves, so I can't believe he's parting with an expensive bottle of wine," Benny said.

Ike came over and asked how the wine tasted. They all complimented him in his wine selection and thanked him for the free bottle.

"Dana, mind if I speak with you privately in my office?" Ike asked, sounding almost embarrassed.

Dana looked at Benny and Courtney and imagined she was sporting the same puzzled expression on her face.

"Of course," she said as she got up and excused herself.

Ike apologized for interrupting their dinner and promised he wouldn't keep her long.

As she followed Ike to his office, the thought that she might be following a killer alone crept through her mind, but he would have to really be off the rails to try something nefarious at his restaurant during busy dining time.

The restaurant's outdoor facade and decor inside were regal-like, which their neo-classical look attempted to convey. It wasn't up to Dana's taste, reminding her of one of the gaudy casinos in Las Vegas more than anything else. She didn't know what to expect of his office, but was surprised that it was rather unremarkable in comparison to the brand Ike was going for. But she figured few guests would find themselves in the office, so Ike wasn't about to spend a lot of money decking it out.

"Sit, please," he said as he sat down on his chair behind his desk. The desk was a flimsy metal desk you could buy for cheap at the office supply box stores. It looked like it was made from the same materials they used to make a tin can of sardines.

Dana sat. "So, what's up, Ike?"

He seemed embarrassed as he poured himself a glass of bourbon.

"It's the cheap stuff, but it's quite good. A nice kick to it, would you like some?" he said, holding up his glass of bourbon.

"No, thank you."

He took a drink.

"I didn't kill Barry Shy."

Dana joined Benny and Courtney back at their table ten minutes later.

"We were starting to worry," Courtney said.

"What did he want to talk to you about?"

"It was a bit awkward, but I just think he needed to talk to someone who would understand what it's like to be falsely suspected of murder," Dana said, taking a big drink from her glass of wine.

She looked around, feeling weird talking about it within earshot of other diners and of Ike's staff.

"So he didn't confess to murder," Courtney said jokingly.

"Not funny, Court," Dana replied. "He's heard the rumor mill working overtime around town about him and Barry. He said they did have a bitter dispute over land access behind his restaurant. Barry's cabin is just a couple miles up the mountain, so he liked to come down and go through his dumpster for recyclables and who knows what else, which made Ike furious to have a disheveled, bearded man going through his garbage, so he put a lock on it, which put Barry on a warpath, causing a lot of disruption to his business. He would come down during busy dinnertime and he would park his trike across the street and yell obscenities at Ike's customers. Ike filed a complaint with the police, but since he wasn't trespassing, they didn't do anything. Ike sprayed him with a hose once, so Barry slashed his tires, although it was never proven he did it. It all came to a head a few weeks before Barry was killed, and they got into a fistfight, which was quickly broken up by the restaurant staff."

"So that's why Picado is sweet on Ike being Barry's killer," Benny said.

"Yes, but it doesn't make sense that he would drive down to Mariposa Beach, break into my store, or somehow confront Barry in my bookstore and kill him there when he could just go up to Barry's cabin and do it there, since it's secluded and hidden away."

"I tend to agree. Doesn't make sense," Benny said.

"He told me he's leaving Costa Rica until this blows over."

"That won't look good at all, and Picado will throw a fit," Benny said.

"He doesn't care. He's afraid that even though he's lived here for decades that he's still seen as a foreigner, so he'll get railroaded for the murder, and he knows the town is gossiping about it, so he needs to get away from it. So he's going to Holland to visit his daughter and grandkids. But he wanted me to know what was going on, since he knows his leaving now will put the Gossip Brigade into overdrive," Dana said.

"Do you think he could be the murderer?" Courtney asked.

"No way," Dana said.

Benny agreed.

They drank their wine and ate their dinner, but the awkwardness of her conversation with Ike made Dana feel a great sense of relief when they were back in Benny's truck, headed back to Casa Verde.

TWENTY-SIX

Dana had been checking her phone for a message from Bucky Moreland obsessively. She did so during dinner at Ike's Oceanview Restaurant the previous night—the checking doubled after her bizarre chat with Ike in his office.

Benny had dropped Dana and Courtney at Casa Verde then headed to his beach house on the other side of town.

Dana and Courtney went to bed soon after. But even after hitting the hay, Dana was awakened a few times, and figured since she was awake, she would check her phone for a message from Bucky, much to the chagrin of Wally, who seemed to be bothered by the blue hue of the phone illuminating the darkness of the bedroom.

The next morning, Dana woke with a headache that she blamed on the wine and banana daiquiris and not on the constant staring into her phone's screen.

Still nada from Bucky Moreland. She figured it wouldn't be easy to track someone down from a single fuzzy phone picture taken from a distance.

Courtney came down as Dana was having a bowl of dry cereal and a cup of coffee. "Good morning."

Courtney grunted and poured herself some coffee. Dana smiled. Ever since they were college roommates, Courtney had never been a morning person.

After showering and getting dressed, Dana headed downstairs to figure out what to do for the day. There had been no word from Bucky or the police about the investigation, which meant her bookstore would be shuttered for another day.

Dana and Courtney decided that today would be about fun. The gloom and doom of Barry Shy's death and the limbo status of her bookstore was wearing them down, and unless Bucky found something good, there wasn't much they could do about it anyway.

Dana was trying to convince Courtney to go on a zip line tour of the jungle. It was a blast to be clipped onto a cable as your body glided above the treetops through the jungle.

"I don't know, sounds like a roller coaster ride without the carts, and you know I don't like roller coaster rides."

Before Dana could reply, her phone buzzed. She looked down. "It's Bucky," she said excitedly. She held the phone tight in her hand as she read his message. "I need to get on my laptop," Dana said as she bolted towards the study.

She returned a couple minutes later holding her laptop in the open position in her hands. She was tapping on its keys as she walked to the living room, where she had left Courtney talking about her fear of roller coasters.

"Well? Did Bucky find anything good?" Courtney asked after a minute of silence.

Dana blinked a few times and nodded slowly before finally looking up from her laptop.

"That good, huh?" Courtney asked.

"Oh yeah, Bucky found it all, Chris Smith's real name, what he does, where he lives."

"Scary what these google-type guys can dig up about people," Courtney said.

Dana shrugged. *She is right, and they can come in handy when I'm doing the digging.*

"So, share," Courtney said.

Dana sat next to her on the couch. "His name isn't Chris Smith, it's Chris Longo. He's from Detroit, not Chicago. And he's not in the book business like he claimed. He's a private investigator with a shady reputation."

Benny arrived just as Dana was telling Courtney what Bucky had dug up. He sat down on the chair across from the sofa where Dana and Courtney were sitting. Dana repeated the latest about Chris Longo, the private investigator.

Benny didn't seem as perplexed about the news as Dana and Courtney had been.

"Okay, that is interesting, but it doesn't mean he's here for nefarious reasons. He could just be here on vacation," Benny said.

"Why give me a fake name and the cockamamie story about being a book collector?"

"I've been a lawyer for over ten years. I can't count how many times I've encountered people using fake names, and that's just the ones I figured out. Even if he's up to no good down here, and believe me, Costa Rica attracts foreign shysters like a moth to a flame, it doesn't mean it has anything to do with you, and certainly not that he had anything to do with Barry's murder."

"Gee, Benny, you should go to work for the Costa Rican tourism board," Dana said, rolling her eyes.

"It's the truth," he said.

"Why are all the shady people coming down here to the tropics?" Courtney asked.

"Same reasons the honest people like to come down here:

great weather, great people, beautiful country, a change of scenery." Benny looked at Dana and smiled.

She looked down at her computer and began looking at more of the data she had received. "According to Bucky, this guy does have a shady reputation. He has been arrested for passing bad checks, stalking, and impersonating a police officer."

"Jeez, how does this creep hold on to his PI license?" Courtney wondered out loud.

"So let's look at this from the angle that he was here for you. Why would a private investigator from Detroit be interested in you?" Benny asked.

Dana mulled it over for a bit. "I have no idea. I've never even been to Detroit, but it's too much of a coincidence that all of a sudden there is a private investigator snooping around my bookstore. A man that gives me a fake name and tells me he's in the book business. I mean, come on, what are the odds he's not here snooping for my books?" Dana asked.

After a moment of silence, Benny, who was seemingly lost in thought, said, "I agree. That would be one heck of a coincidence, especially after discovering those valuable books that were hidden away by your uncle."

"Weren't you working with a book expert to figure out the value of those books?" Courtney asked.

"Yes, Greyson Bay, but he's in New York City, and he has a good reputation in the business. How would he get mixed up with a creepy PI from Detroit, and what would he have to gain anyway?"

"Maybe he hired this guy to steal your books," Courtney said.

"No, not him, he runs a bookstore, he's just a book nerd."

"Or maybe he knows Chris Longo and he told him about it, you know, sort of off the cuff, this woman down in the middle of nowhere, Costa Rica is sitting on a fortune of books, so this crooked PI thinks to himself, *interesting*, and he books a flight down here to see if he can get his hands on those books," Benny said.

"I could see that happening," Dana said.

"Why don't you ask Greyson if he knows Chris Longo?" Courtney asked.

Benny shifted in his chair like he had been poked with a hot iron.

"Let's not act too hasty right now. If they are in cahoots, the last thing we need is tipping off Greyson Bay that we know about Chris Longo."

"And how does Barry Shy fit into this all? The man is practically a hermit living in a cabin without electricity or indoor plumbing, I doubt he would know or be involved with someone like Chris Longo or even Greyson," Dana said.

"That is true. If Chris Longo really was in town to steal your books, I can't imagine Barry getting wrapped up in something like that, especially for money, because Barry might have been a lot of things, but no one would say he was a thief. The man loathed money and greed with a passion."

They were quiet for what seemed to Dana was an hour, but it was just a moment.

"So what now?" she asked, crossing her arms in frustration.

"Can you ask Bucky to look into Greyson Bay?" Benny asked.

Now it was Dana's turn to shift in her seat like she had been poked with a hot iron. She liked Greyson Bay. He had been very helpful to her, and she felt it was wrong to snoop in on him. Chris Longo, her loudmouth stalker, was fair game in her book. But Greyson? It seemed he was a line in the sand that she didn't want to cross.

"I don't know, that seems a bit 'backstabby.'"

"First we determine if he really has a good reputation in the book business like you've been told, then we can see if there is a connection between him and Chris Longo," Benny said.

"Jeez, now I'm the one feeling like a sleazy private investigator," Dana said, picking up her mobile phone to FaceTime Bucky.

TWENTY-SEVEN

Dana woke up the next morning feeling anxious, so she meditated for twenty minutes. Her phone rang, snapping her out of her meditative trance. Although she usually put her phone in airplane mode when meditating, she wanted to keep the line open in case Bucky called. She excitedly picked up her phone, but it was not a call from Bucky's 650 area code. It was Detective Gabriela Rojas. Dana tensed up a little. Even though she liked Rojas, it was unnerving to have the police call you during an investigation.

But this time, the detective had good news. She informed Dana that they were finally done working the crime scene, aka her bookstore, and Picado had authorized its release. She had her bookstore back.

Rojas informed Dana that of course Picado—being the way he was—could have released the scene a few days ago, but he refused even though the forensic investigators, the medical examiner, and his supervisor had signed off on it. Rojas had been pushing him to do the right thing, but for whatever reason he was pigheaded until finally relenting a few minutes before she called Dana.

"Why would he do that?" Dana asked Rojas.

"It's just the way he is. I don't know what happened to him along the way to make him so gruff. But finally today he knew he couldn't justify it any longer to our boss. Your lawyer, Benny Campos, was calling every day, putting pressure on him."

That made Dana smile. She had no idea Benny had been calling the police on her behalf.

"What a jerk," Dana said with a snort.

"No comment," Rojas told Dana with a snicker.

She thanked the detective and hung up, then she screamed out for Courtney, who came bolting from her room. "What's going on?" she asked, worried.

"Sorry, didn't mean to freak you out, it's just that I'm so excited. That was Detective Rojas on the phone. They're done with my bookstore. It's all mine again."

They squealed in excitement as they hugged and jumped up and down like tweens at a K-pop concert.

"Let me get my keys. I want to get in there right away," Dana said.

"I haven't even showered yet," Courtney protested.

"Me either, just grab a T-shirt and put on a hat if you're worried about your hair," Dana said as she ran up the stairs.

Dana slapped on some light makeup, then she put her hair in a low ponytail. She grabbed her San Francisco Giants baseball hat and put her ponytail through the back opening of the cap. She put on a T-shirt, slipped into khaki shorts and flip-flops, and in less than five minutes she was downstairs, ready and chomping at the bit to go.

"You coming?" she shouted towards the guest room from downstairs. She was standing by the front door, tapping her foot impatiently.

"Just a sec," Courtney yelled from the other side of the closed door.

Fifteen minutes after hanging up the phone with Detective Rojas, Dana pulled up to Ark Row and parked in front of her store.

It was a surreal experience to be standing there. It was still on the early side of the morning, but the air was already thick and wet from the tropical humidity. She had been living there long enough to know it was going to be another scorcher of a day in the tropics.

As she parked, a nice cooling breeze from the Pacific Ocean blew past them. It felt good to Dana's skin. Those little bursts of wind from the Pacific felt wonderful on a hot, sticky day.

They got out of the jeep and Dana looked up at her bookstore's signage that swayed in the wind. Her eyes welled up looking at it—Mariposa Books.

For the first time in a week, there wasn't yellow crime scene tape everywhere.

Courtney squeezed her hand. "Come on, let's go check out your bookstore, I've been dying to see it... oh, poor choice of words, sorry."

The looked at each other for a moment and then burst out laughing. "We shouldn't laugh; it's a bit macabre. But that was the worst choice of words you could have used." They burst out laughing again.

Once they regained their composure, they walked up to the front door. Dana unlocked the metal curtain that rolled down to protect the front door from thieves. *Little good that did, when they just busted in from the back,* Dana thought as she undid the lock and rolled the metal curtain up as it clanked loudly.

She was nervous to go inside for the first time since she found Barry Shy's lifeless body sprawled out on her floor.

Big Mike popped out of his surf shop in his usual attire of longboard shorts and a white sleeveless T-shirt.

"Hey you two, pura vida," he shouted as he walked over towards Dana and Courtney.

"Hey, Big Mike. The police finally said it was okay to go inside."

"Yeah, man, I saw Freddy remove the police tape this morning. He said Picado gave the okay to release the crime scene, then I saw you pull in with Big Red and I was like booya, Dana's back."

"I'm back all right. I just need to figure out when I can open for business."

"Open up right away. Shut up the naysayers."

"Naysayers? Who's naysaying?"

Big Mike cringed like he just told Virginia that there actually wasn't a Santa Claus.

He hemmed and hawed for a moment, shuffling his Keen sandals, tugging on his T-shirt.

"Mike, I'm a big girl, you can tell me," Dana said, hands on her hips.

"She was a thick-skinned, nosy reporter for one of the biggest newspapers in California. Gossip bounces off her like a little kid in a bounce house," Courtney added for good measure.

"It's dumb, basically that like, you're cursed or you just have rotten bad luck and people drop dead around you like flies in a zapper."

"What have you heard about Barry's death? Any rumors coming from the Gossip Brigade on that?"

"Same old bull, I'm afraid." He stopped to think about it some more and he smiled. "Oh, there is one more thing that's new and pretty juicy, I might add," Big Mike said, grinning ear to ear.

"I'm afraid to ask," Dana said.

"I'm not. Spill the tea, Big Mike," Courtney said loudly.

Big Mike leaned closer and whispered into Dana's ear so close that she could feel his breath in her ear.

She recoiled back and said, "Oh, that's just disgusting and idiotic."

"I warned you," he said as he turned back to walk to his store. "Let me know if you need anything, like borrowing a cup of sugar. I'm your good neighbor," Big Mike said, laughing at his own joke and going back to his surf shop.

"You're a good guy, Big Mike," Dana said as he walked away.

"Don't leave me hanging. What did he tell you?" Courtney asked.

"That Barry and I had a thing, and one thing led to another and he winds up dead. A lovers' quarrel, I guess," Dana said, shaking her head.

"Oh, gross."

"I wholeheartedly agree. I'm not going to let the town gossip wreck this moment," Dana said, dangling the keys to the bookstore's front door in the air.

She put the key into the door's lock and turned. Click. Unlocked. She had probably heard that sound a million times in her lifetime, but on that day it was music to her ears.

"I don't want to think about that or the case right now, I just want to step inside my bookstore and get this bad boy ready for show time," Dana said as she stepped inside.

TWENTY-EIGHT

It was dark inside. Dana and Courtney walked in on their tiptoes. She felt like they were Nancy Drew and Bess Marvin on the trail to solve a mystery.

She turned on the lights and she half expected the place to be coated in thick dust and cobwebs, but that was her mind making things seem worse in her head.

It had been less than a week since she had last been inside her bookstore as she prepared for the big grand opening which had come and gone.

The bookstore was pretty much as she had left it on that day. She was also pleasantly surprised the police hadn't ransacked the place.

"This looks pretty normal. I thought it would be tossed and covered in that fingerprint powder stuff," Courtney said, breaking Dana from her thoughts.

"Me too," Dana said, sounding relieved.

"So... where was... you know... the body."

Dana realized she had avoided even looking in that direction. "Over there, behind the counter," she pointed with her chin, shoving her hands deep into her short pockets.

Courtney slowly walked towards the counter. Dana followed her. They hesitantly peered over the counter, which Dana thought was foolish. It's not like the police would have left Barry's dead body lying where she had found him.

Courtney glanced at Dana, who shrugged.

"I'll be honest, and not to get all ghoulish, but I thought maybe there would be blood stains that we would need to clean up."

Dana looked closer just in case, but the floor looked clean, vacuumed, even, and she wondered if the police actually tidied up after themselves. She shook that thought from her mind. It was time to focus on the store.

Dana and Courtney spent a couple hours at the bookstore doing inventory and cleaning. Not that she thought the police would be stealing ten-dollar paperbacks. And even though Detective Picado had matched all books in her database to make sure none were missing, Dana went through the inventory herself on her laptop and she came to the same conclusion as Picado: every book was accounted for.

"I don't understand what went down here."

"It has the cops stumped, so don't beat yourself up over it. Who knows what possesses a human being to kill another human being."

Dana was impressed at Courtney waxing all philosophical.

"What?" she asked defensively as Dana smiled.

"Nothing."

Word traveled fast in Mariposa Beach. Within an hour of arriving at the bookstore, Dana had already chatted with Big Mike, who seemed to double as the National Warning System, because Mindy came bearing coffee and pineapple empanadas.

"Big Mike stopped by for his coffee fix and he said you were here, why didn't you tell me you were coming?" Mindy glanced over at Courtney. Mindy had become close to Dana since Dana moved to Mariposa Beach, and she seemed to feel a tinge of jealousy the few times she had met Courtney, and it appeared to Dana that the feeling was mutual, as Courtney referred to Mindy as her stand-in covering the friendship gap when she was back home in San Francisco. *My Costa Rica-Me* she would say jokingly, but not to Mindy.

"Detective Rojas called me out of the blue, and we just came straight over. I didn't really put much thought into it. When I was given the all-clear by the police, I jumped into Big Red and sped on over here."

There was a knock on the door. Dana hesitantly went to the door to see who was there. It seemed like the whole town was in snooping mode, which was not that unusual.

"Maybe it's him," Courtney whispered.

"Who?"

"Chris Longo," she whispered even lower.

"Who's Chris Longo?" Mindy asked.

"My loudmouth stalker," Dana said walking towards the door.

"I thought his name was Chris Smith," Mindy said sounding confused.

"He was using a fake name," Courtney chimed in.

"I'll fill you in on the latest," Dana said opening the door.

To Dana's surprise, it was Doña Chilla of the Gossip Brigade with a bag of groceries from the market across the street.

"I saw that pretty red Jeep of yours parked out front. I thought I would stop by to say hello," she said, peering inside, stealing a look inside of the shuttered store. "The police finally gave you permission to open?" she asked, still looking around.

"Yes, finally. Have you heard anything about the police's investigation?"

Dana tried to figure out the latest rumblings and musings in town about her bookstore, but Doña Chilla seemed offended that she would be asked such a question.

"How would I know?" the old lady said, sounding vexed. If she had been wearing a pearl necklace, she would have probably clutched the pearls.

"I didn't mean to offend you, it just seems that when something happens in town, your canasta-playing crew finds out about it," Dana said with a smile.

The old lady smiled, feeling important. "Well," she finally said. "My grandson's wife's brother's girlfriend is Officer Freddy Sanchez's cousin, and they're very close. They grew up together in Filadelfia," Doña Chilla said then stopped, having noticed Dana's confused face. "Filadelfia in the Guanacaste province, not Philadelphia in America," she explained.

Dana felt embarrassed, and she smiled and shrugged her shoulders. Courtney laughed. "That's what I thought you meant."

"I had no idea there was a Philadelphia in Costa Rica."

"*Filadelfia*," Doña Chilla corrected her.

"Anyway. Freddy's mother, Doña Flor, is such a wonderful lady, she raised him and his three brothers and two cousins all by herself. Her husband, Don Hector, was a drunk. He was trying to stumble home one night from the bar and he was hit by a truck and died. He was a bum anyway. Poor Doña Flor had to support everyone. He was a drunk."

You mentioned that, Dana thought. The old lady had a habit of repeating herself often. But she instead said, "She sounds like a wonderful, strong woman, but what did you hear about the dead man in my bookstore?"

The old lady looked around just in case Detective Picado or Officer Freddy were hiding behind a bookshelf. "Freddy told his cousins, who then told—"

Dana interrupted her, "What did he tell his cousin?"

The old lady straightened herself out and she wrinkled her nose at Dana's directness.

"What I heard is that the police doesn't believe Barry had anything to do with breaking into your store. They believe that someone else broke into it and he just happened to be riding by on that bicycle contraption of his, so he stopped to check it out. Cost that poor man's life."

Doña Chilla left soon after sharing that tidbit of gossip and with a couple of Mindy's pineapple empanadas.

Once she was gone, Dana gave Courtney a quizzical look. "Now tell me this shady PI isn't involved in all this somehow."

"It seems like it would be a heck of a coincidence. You think he's after those first-edition books?"

"The only way he would know is if Greyson Bay told him, but I can't imagine he'd be wrapped up in something like this. A thief. A murderer? No way."

"I doubt they planned to kill Barry. Especially after what Doña Chilla said. He might have just stumbled upon malfeasance."

"It sounds like he was just in the wrong place at the wrong time. That poor fool."

Benny arrived at the bookstore about twenty minutes after Doña Chilla left. Dana had texted him the good news about her bookstore opening and how she and Courtney were rushing over there.

"I got your text," Benny said, walking into the store. "It's so great to see you in your store."

Dana and Courtney were quieter than usual.

"What's up?" he asked. He must have sensed something had happened.

Dana filled him in with the latest news from Doña Chilla.

Benny mulled it over, and she could see him thinking about the words he was about to speak, something lawyers usually did.

"Well," he finally said, "it does seem like Chris Longo was looking to rip you off. But I wouldn't jump to conclusions or start thinking that there is this big conspiracy to steal your first editions. I've dealt with many shady characters that come to Costa Rica, and these types of people have a nose for opportunities to make a quick buck, and the only calculation to go through their head on whether or not to pounce is the probability of getting caught. So Longo is here on vacation or for some other reason on his own, and he comes upon your soon-to-open bookstore. He meets you. Finds out that you're a new expat and that you're opening a brand new bookstore with inventory from your uncle's book collection you inherited, and the criminal wheels start turning. We've all heard of the person that buys a thirty-million-dollar Picasso at a garage sale for five bucks. So Longo thinks, maybe that's the case here. Maybe he does know about books, and he looks around at little old sleepy Mariposa Beach. He finds out the closest cop is a dirt bike-riding tourist cop and he's fifteen miles away. It's easy pickings and worth breaking into to see if there is anything of value he could steal."

Dana thought about it. It seemed possible.

"And then poor old crazy Barry Shy stumbles into a burglary in progress," Dana adds.

Benny nods his head. "Like I said, I know these types, it's like cornering a wild animal. They will lash out to break free. Barry has no idea what he's up against. This man pulls his knife and..." Benny trails off, not wanting to describe the old hippy's untimely manner of death.

"We need to find Chris Longo."

"Um, no, Detectives Picado and Rojas need to find Chris Longo, not us. Please, Dana, let the police do their job. Call

Detective Rojas and let her know about the first-edition angle," Benny pleaded.

"Yes, please, Dana. Benny just said that people like Chris Longo are like wild animals willing to strike back if they feel cornered. And us finding him and asking questions about all this is doing just that. He might react the same way and lash out like he did with Barry. It's too risky," Courtney added.

"We don't even know if that's what happened," Dana said dismissively.

"I would imagine the reason you haven't been able to find him is because he's long gone. You don't kill someone and hang around the scene of the crime for too long. I would imagine he's back in Detroit by now," Benny said.

Dana agreed. It made sense.

"Okay, okay, you guys are right. I'll call Detective Rojas."

Dana saw Benny look at Courtney and smile in relief.

"What?" Dana asked.

"He can't believe you're listening to him for once," Courtney said with a big grin.

"Oh, shush," Dana said, smiling.

"I didn't say a word," Benny said, holding up his hands in the air. Dana reached for her telephone.

"By the way, when I talked to Rojas this morning, she told me you were calling Picado as my lawyer, putting a fire under his feet to release my bookstore as a crime scene. Thank you."

Benny smiled and blushed a little. "My pleasure."

Dana looked at Courtney, who stood there with a big, wide, goofy grin on her face. Dana rolled her eyes at her as she dug out the detective's business card from her purse.

On the blank side of the card she had jotted down her mobile phone number. Dana decided to call her on her cell phone to avoid any chance that Picado might answer the phone if she called the station.

She picked up after a few rings.

"Rojas," her voice barked, sounding monotone and serious, not her usual tone. It caused Dana to tense up a bit and think *What now?*

TWENTY-NINE

Dana recovered from the brisk tone in Rojas's voice that very much sounded like she was bothering her. She cleared her throat.

"Detective Rojas, it's Dana."

"Yes, hello, Dana, what is it?" Rojas said. She wasn't being friendly as usual, but was sounding curt, like Dana was interrupting her. Dana went ahead and laid it out all on the table. She told Rojas what she had found out about Chris Longo and the interest he had in getting into her store to look through her books.

"It was creepy and unnerving. Not like a normal book fan. He's like stalking me, and he scares me."

"Yes, we know all about Mr. Longo. He was our prime suspect."

"Was? Did you clear him?"

"We're actually heading down your way. There has been a development in the case and we needed to talk to you anyway. Where are you going to be between three thirty and four p.m.?"

Dana looked at her watch. It was one o'clock. "I'll be at home in Casa Verde."

"Okay, we'll see you there." The phone call disconnected.

Odd. "They're coming down from Nicoya to talk to me about a development in the case. She said Chris Longo *was* their prime suspect," Dana said, sounding ominous.

"Maybe they already arrested the guy," Courtney said.

"No, she would have told me that. Looks like they cleared him. They must have checked his alibi or whatever and it checked out. So it wasn't him," Dana said, sounding disappointed.

"Well, we'll find out soon enough. Let's grab some lunch and head back to Casa Verde," Benny said, checking the time on his iPhone.

The mood was a bit dour as they ate at the Qué Vista Restaurant. Jorge, the affable head waiter and manager, must have picked up on the somber vibe in comparison to the usual vibrant and happy group.

He brought them three ice-cold Imperial beers and he told him they were on the house.

And that did cheer them up. Funny how the little things, like a five-dollar beer for free, could be so uplifting.

Their food arrived, and they mostly ate in silence. Benny ate a steak casado. Dana had the chicken casado, and Courtney the arroz con pollo.

"Come on, guys, maybe it's good news," Courtney said after a long stretch of silent eating.

"Even if it's great news, when I have to face Picado, I get depressed."

Benny smiled. "He has that effect on people."

"Well, at least we're not too depressed to eat. The food is always so good here," Courtney said as she put a spoonful of the delicious dish into her mouth.

After lunch, Dana drove back to Casa Verde with Courtney in Big Red. Benny followed. His big Land Cruiser SUV looked like it could easily run over the small Willys Jeep like one of those big monster trucks at one of those car-crunching derby shows on television. Sunday... Sunday... Sunday... the voice of the eager and overexcited announcer screaming over the television set filled her head.

At four thirty, Dana received a text from Detective Rojas: *be there in ten minutes.*

"That's her, they'll be here soon," Dana said to Courtney and Benny as she looked out her large bay window which overlooked the front garden and down the gravel driveway that led down to the front gate. Ramón was outside, watering. He smiled and waved at Dana. She returned the wave.

The front-gate ringer buzzed. Dana ran over to the monitor installed by the front door. Even though Ramón and Carmen lived on the property, their house sat back over sixty yards away. In a small town like Mariposa Beach, it wouldn't take long for word to get out that a single expat female lived there alone, so she replaced her uncle's old front-gate ringer with a state-of-the-art, wall-mounted color monitor that offered a crisp high-definition video image of the person or persons ringing the bell outside. It was also audio-enabled, so she could also hear and speak to whoever was outside her gate.

She could see the white Nissan Versa and Detective Gabriela Rojas sitting behind the wheel, resting her left arm on the doorframe of the car as she waved at the camera. Picado sat on the passenger side looking straight ahead, looking annoyed as usual.

Dana pushed the intercom button and said, "Come on in." Then she pressed the button that opened the front gate.

The three of them greeted the detectives at the front door. Dana offered them something to drink, which they declined. As usual, Detective Rojas was pleasant and charming. Detective Picado was stoic and was only able to grunt out a dismissive hello when she said hi. He made it almost impossible to even attempt to be cordial with him.

She remembered saying to Benny months ago during the investigation of her cousin Roy's murder that Picado seemed to not like her very much. "Not even just dislike, he seems to loathe me," she had said back then.

"Don't take it personally, he treats everyone equally bad, but deep down that nastiness, he's a good detective," Benny had said.

That might be true, Dana thought as Picado sat on her living room chair and scowled at her, but he made it very hard for her not to take it personally.

"So what's going on?" Dana finally asked after everyone settled into their chairs in the living room.

Detective Rojas looked at Picado. He gave her a *go ahead* nod.

"As you're aware, the name of Mr. Chris Longo of Detroit, Michigan, has come up a few times during the course of our investigation into the murder of Mr. Barry Shy."

I know all that. Get there. Faster, Dana said to herself, hoping she had telepathic powers that Rojas would pick up on. She didn't, so she just nodded impatiently.

"We heard that he was pestering you and was very insistent at getting into your bookstore to look at your books. Obviously that got our attention. So we interviewed him and found he was being evasive, which of course made us look closer into his background, and we found some unsavory dealings with the Detroit police in his background, so we decided to bring him in for further questioning."

"That's great, I couldn't find him in town," Dana said, immediately regretting it.

"Why were you looking for him?" Picado snapped.

"He was so adamant about wanting to see my book inventory that I wanted to let him know that hopefully I would be opening my bookstore soon, so he could come in and have a look," Dana lied. It was a good save, but she doubted Picado believed her. Then again, she didn't care.

Courtney and Benny shifted in their chairs at the same time.

Picado's eyes darted towards them. Dana noticed he was always very observant. She imagined that to a trained and experienced homicide investigator like Picado, every little move, shift, placement of the hands, feet, or lick of the lips was a treasure trove of information for him. He turned his attention back to Dana.

"Okay, so you say."

"Whatever, Detective, I know you don't like me, I don't really care. Did you bring Chris Longo in for more questioning? Have you arrested him? What do you want with me?" she snapped angrily. She could feel Benny looking at her, and she could imagine him shouting Nooo! like Darth Vader.

Picado seemed taken aback, and it seemed to Dana that he might have been impressed with her standing up to him, but maybe that's how she had replayed their little exchange.

"The reason you haven't been able to find him to give him the good news about your bookstore opening," Picado said, so facetiously that Dana wanted to punch him in the nose, but she needed to assault a police officer like she needed a hole in her head, "is because Mr. Longo is in our morgue up in San José."

"He's d-dead?" Dana stammered.

"I don't know how they do things in the United States, but in Costa Rica the morgue is where we keep our dead bodies."

"I don't think such sarcasm is appropriate, Detective," Benny snapped.

"Do you think meddling in my investigations, despite multiple warnings to butt out, is appropriate?"

"Look—"

Picado waved him off.

"It does appear that Mr. Longo and Mr. Shy broke into your store. For reasons we'll never know, since both men are now deceased. For whatever reason, Mr. Longo turned on Mr. Shy and killed him. The day after we talked to him about the murder, he took a bus to San José. He was staying in the red light district, partaking in the entertainment provided there before his flight back to Detroit the next day. He was walking down a bad part of town alone at two in the morning when he was shot during a mugging gone bad. Why people insist on fighting back versus just giving up their wallet is beyond me, but in this case, karma caught up with Mr. Longo."

Dana, Courtney, and Benny sat there dumbfounded for a moment.

"Did the police catch the killer?"

"No. Not yet." Picado and Rojas seemed annoyed and embarrassed.

"The forensic team is on it right now. He was shot with a Bersa three hundred eighty, an Argentinian pistol that is popular with local criminals," Picado added as he brushed lint off his pants leg. "We'll find his killer soon enough," he added.

"So what happens now?" Dana asked.

"As far as I'm concerned, the case is closed," Picado said, getting up from his chair.

Dana was stunned. *Can it be that straightforward?* She sure hoped Picado was right.

THIRTY

Courtney had extended her visit by three days, so she was packing her suitcase to head back to San Francisco before she got fired.

"I'm going to miss you, kiddo," Dana said as she lay on the bed of the guest room, petting Wally's head as they watched Courtney pack.

"Me too. So, when are you leaving the tropics to visit me in San Francisco?"

"I have a new business to get off the ground, so realistically, it probably won't be for a few months."

"Makes sense. I don't like it, but it makes sense."

"Benny will be here soon."

"You don't have to tag along, Dana. You're busy, and Benny was heading back to San José anyway, so he can drop me off at the airport."

"I'm not missing out on seeing you off. Besides, after everything that happened, I'm looking forward to staying the night in a big city. My grand-opening day has come and gone. Another day or two won't make a difference."

Courtney flashed a wide smile. Dana knew she liked it

when she let her hair down and stopped being uptight about self-imposed deadlines and goals.

"So why a hotel? Benny doesn't have a guest room at his place up there?" Courtney grinned.

"He did offer his guest room, but I prefer to not make things more complicated than they need to be. Besides, he has to work in the morning. I want to hit the mall in Escazú, and the hotel is right across the street."

Courtney looked at her disapprovingly. "How are you going to get back, then?"

"I'm already booked for tomorrow's afternoon flight with Captain Junior," Dana said, smiling, knowing how much Courtney hated flying in his little plane.

"He's a nice guy. And heck, he must be a great pilot to not crash that little paper plane of his into the side of the mountain, but I'm glad we're driving back up to the city," Courtney said.

"Well, come back soon and I'll pick you up so you don't have to fly down with Captain Junior."

The drive from Mariposa Beach to the Juan Santamaría International Airport, which was located in Alajuela, the second-largest city in Costa Rica after the capital, San José, took almost five hours because of bad traffic. The other international airport is the Daniel Oduber Quirós airport in Liberia. It's closer but not as many flights and it would be out of Benny's way since he was heading to San José.

The Costa Rican highway system was mostly a two-lane road which was jam-packed with cars, semi-trucks, buses, and Dana was convinced, with bat-crazy drivers on a death wish. A lot of the tico drivers were certifiable, as far as she was concerned.

At the airport, they said their goodbyes. Dana watched Courtney walk into the terminal with her luggage with tears welling up in her eyes.

Back in the Land Cruiser, Benny said, "She's a wonderful friend."

"She really is. It's crazy, but I miss her already like she's been gone a month. I don't have any siblings, so she's like my sister."

"It's a thing of beauty to have a friendship like that," Benny said, putting the SUV into drive and pulled away from the terminal.

Dana felt a nice sense of calm wash over her until they pulled into the madness of Costa Rican traffic.

The airport wasn't far from Escazú, but it took them almost an hour in heavy traffic to get there.

"I miss the empty streets of Mariposa Beach, potholes included," Dana said, looking out the window.

Escazú was a suburb of San José, and it was ground zero for the expat community and the well-off. Benny grew up in the Escazú Province when it used to be a pasture for horses and cattle, which seemed hard to believe looking at the built-up grid-locked city which now teemed with tall office buildings and large homes behind high security walls or in gated communities protected by armed guards.

Buildings brimming with expensive condos and office spaces dotted the hillsides. It was also a shopping mecca with malls of all shapes and sizes scattered throughout Avenida Escazú.

"Welcome to the Beverly Hills of Costa Rica," Benny said, smiling at the cheesy nickname given to Escazú by expats.

Dana smiled thinly.

She had been to his office before, which was located near the MultiPlaza Mall. It was a small but very nice office for his solo practice. The office building shared a common reception area and conference rooms with the other tenants—mostly lawyers and accountants. So it was perfect for him.

They drove down by the Sabana Park, San José's version of San Francisco's Golden Gate Park, down a long, winding road that connected to the Puente de los Anonos, a bridge over the Tiribí River that served as the old road from La Sabana to Escazú which bypassed the highway.

"It's a toss-up, but sometimes there is less traffic and hassle this way," Benny explained as he drove.

After crossing the bridge, he drove for another few minutes before turning off the main road to a side street, driving by what looked like a sprawling campus and golf course.

"That's the Costa Rican Country Club. Nice, but snobby," he explained as he drove past it.

"Looks beautiful."

A few minutes later he drove down a steep road.

"Now this reminds me of San Francisco."

"The way the prices keep going up in Escazú, it's going to feel more like San Francisco," Benny said.

He continued to drive before offering again for her to stay at his house to avoid paying for a hotel. She knew his intentions were pure, but she declined. It would be too awkward, and she would feel uncomfortable staying at his place. The sterile and impersonal surroundings of a hotel actually beckoned to her.

After about ten minutes, Benny pulled into the front lobby of the hotel.

"Well, I'll let you get to it," he said as he came around. He always tried to open the door for her, but she wasn't used to that and always forgot, and then they stood there awkwardly for a moment. And it happened again as they both laughed nervously.

Dana had begun to drift into sleep when her mobile phone rang. It was almost eleven thirty at night. She looked at the caller ID and it was Bucky.

Dana thought that either he forgot that California was two hours behind of Costa Rica or he had something very important to call about.

"Hey, Bucky."

"Hey, did I wake you?"

"Nah, I just lay down and was just starting to drift away, but I'm awake, what's up?"

"I found a lot more information about Chris Longo, and I think it's very important that you know as soon as possible. I know you're a couple hours ahead time-wise, but you'll want to hear about this, since I think that dude is quite dangerous."

"You don't have to worry about him hurting me. He's dead."

"Whoa, how?"

"According to the police, he went to the red light district, which can be quite dangerous for a drunken tourist, as you can imagine, and he was robbed, but he fought back and was killed by a mugger."

"How awful. At least I don't have to worry about having that guy running around under the same area code as you."

"I just wish I knew what he was up to."

"Well, I will provide you with some more information on the type of stuff he was usually up to, because it's a pattern."

Dana sat up in bed and turned on the nightstand lamp.

"Okay, what did you find out?"

"Chris Longo had quite the criminal history, which led the state to yank his PI license almost two years ago."

"So he wasn't even licensed?"

"Nope. He was a black market PI with a reputation for filling custom burglary jobs."

"Custom burglary jobs, what the heck do you mean?"

"It's fascinating murky waters that cat swam in. It's like right out of an Elmore Leonard novel. Let's say I want an Andy Warhol painting that's part of a private collection. Well, I could hire Chris Longo to steal it for me. I talked to a cop in the Detroit PD, and he said that they were onto him for stealing high-end vehicles from Michigan and the Midwest, which he would then ship off to Eastern Europe and Latin America, so he was familiar with your neck of the woods. And from what I could find out, Longo's idea of a fun vacation was a gambling junket to Las Vegas or debauchery in that seedy red light district you mentioned, not hitting the beaches of Costa Rica."

"That's the vibe I picked up from him. Creepy," Dana said.

"So why was he in Costa Rica? In that little beach town of yours, no less. I don't think he was there for the white-sand beach you keep telling me about."

"He was very interested in my bookstore."

"It could all be a coincidence. It's not like you had a Picasso hanging in there, did you?"

Dana chuckled. "No, but my uncle had a very valuable collection of first-edition books which now belong to me. But he wouldn't know about that. It's not like I had them up on the bookshelf for sale. My friend Benny has them secured in a safe in San José."

"You told me about those books. Weren't you having them appraised?"

"Yes," Dana said as the wheels were turning in her head.

"Well, I don't mean to freak you out. I highly doubt the appraiser would be mixed up in anything that sordid," Bucky said.

"How can we be so sure?" Dana said. "Chris Longo special-

ized in stealing valuable stuff on special order. I have those valuable books. The appraiser knows how valuable they are down to
the penny. He knows I'm down here alone in a tiny beach town
because like a dolt, I told him. Maybe he thought it was too good
of an opportunity to pass up. He knows about Chris Longo, so
he hires him to go down there and steal my books on his behalf.
So Longo breaks into my store, but then Barry Shy walks into
his burglary in progress and things spiral out of control and he
ends up dead."

"I don't know, I guess anything is possible," Bucky said.
"What's the book expert's name?"

"Greyson Bay."

"All right. I'll pull an all-nighter if I have to, but I'm going to
tear into the life of Greyson Bay starting right after I hang up
the phone. I'll call you in the morning."

"Thanks, Bucky."

"Be careful, Dana."

"I will."

THIRTY-ONE

The next morning, Dana was still feeling creepy about her conversation about Greyson Bay with Bucky. But she decided to proceed with her day as planned. She wasn't going to let any more bad juju get in her way, so she made a spa appointment at the hotel, where she enjoyed being pampered for an hour. She went back to her hotel room and showered, then went downstairs to the restaurant for breakfast.

After that, she did one of the most dangerous activities possible in the city: she walked across the street, dodging cars and buses to get to the mall.

At Starbucks, she ordered a coffee. It struck her that it had been months since she had been to Starbucks, since they didn't have one in Mariposa Beach and they were not on every corner in the Guanacaste Province like they were in the big cities. The coffee was good, but Mindy's was better.

She then spent a couple hours shopping, but it was mostly window-shopping. It dawned on her that she really didn't need what they had for sale at the mall, since down on the beach it really was a simpler life. But it was fun to be back in the hustle and bustle of a crowded city for at least a couple hours.

She took an Uber from the mall to a small municipal airport in San José, where Captain Junior greeted her warmly. There was a couple from Missouri on the flight as well. They were staying in Nosara, but Dana told them all about Mariposa Beach.

She spoke to them about the quiet little beach community and the calm waters courtesy of the Nicoya Peninsula, Mindy's gourmet coffee where the beans were sourced from her husband's family's farm and the bagels and cream cheese that were homemade from scratch. And how her used-book store would be opening in the next few days. She felt excited about heading back home. It surprised her that she was actually missing the little, weird beach town with its nosey and oddball locals.

The tourists seemed excited to drop in for a visit during their week's stay in Nosara. Dana felt guilty for not mentioning the murder, but it was not like New York City or San Francisco talked up their murders with prospective tourists.

It was another white-knuckle flight from the capital down to the coast as the little Cessna bounced in the air like one of those spaceships on a string in *Plan 9 from Outer Space*. But Captain Junior got them there safely, and in forty minutes versus four to five hours in traffic. *Worth the bumpy flight*, Dana thought.

Benny had client work that day, but she had told him all about Bucky's findings. He felt awful about not being able to come down with her.

"Don't be silly," Dana told him.

"As soon as I wrap up my client meeting and the closing I have to attend, I'll head down," Benny said.

"You don't have to do that, Benny, I'm fine."

"I don't have to, but I want to, so I'll see you tomorrow morning."

Dana thanked him. She was actually excited about seeing him again so soon.

Ramón was kind enough to come pick her up at the Nosara Airport in his little pickup. They chitchatted about the good yuca roots he had dug out of the ground and chopped up with his machete and about a landscaping idea he had for a green patch by the front gate. She enjoyed talking to him about Casa Verde instead of the bookstore, Barry Shy, Chris Longo, and customized burglary jobs that made her skin crawl.

She had just gotten back home and was apologizing to Wally for being gone for the night when her phone rang. She looked at the screen. It was Bucky.

He got right into it.

"There were a few shoddy dealings in Greyson Bay's history, that's for sure."

Dana felt a lump in her throat.

"A couple jams for receiving stolen property, which you would be surprised to know isn't that uncommon for folks in his line of work dealing with collectibles. He played dumb. Claimed he had no idea they were stolen. Police couldn't prove he knew, so they let him walk. There was also a case where three men were arrested for roughing up an old man for his very valuable baseball card collection. The police picked them up and the motley crew began to sing like a canary, and they said they were hired by none other than Chris Longo, who they said had been hired by some man in New York City who dealt in collectibles to rip off the old man from his valuable baseball cards."

"What?"

"The name Greyson Bay didn't come up, but what are the odds that it wasn't him that hired Chris Longo for that job?"

"Seems he has a history of staying behind the scenes, pulling the strings for his capers," Dana said.

"It works. I don't see anything showing that Longo told the police about Greyson Bay, so again he emerged unscathed."

Dana felt like she was going to throw up.

Bucky asked Dana to forward him all the emails that she had been exchanging with Greyson Bay so he could check into him even deeper. As soon as Dana recovered from the queasy feeling over trusting a man with a checkered past with her uncle's valuable books, she emailed that information to Bucky. Then she called Benny and told him everything.

"What is Bucky hoping to find by perusing your emails with Greyson?" Benny asked.

"I don't know what he does or how he finds out about this stuff, but if anyone can find the proof to nail that sorry SOB, it's Bucky."

"Not much could be done with him in New York and you being all the way over here," Benny said.

"That's what had Bucky so worried. What if Greyson came down to Costa Rica with Chris Longo to rob me? Maybe he's still down here."

"Mariposa Azul Beach is too small. You would have seen him or someone would have noticed the new face around town. You know how that works now. The Mariposa Azul Beach grapevine would have been all over new faces to gossip about."

Dana chuckled, knowing he was right. And she hoped he was right and that Greyson Bay was still in New York City and had been pulling the strings from there this whole time. Hopefully after hearing about what happened to Chris Longo, he would stay far away from her and her books.

But if Greyson Bay was involved, that meant he was responsible for Barry Shy's death, since he was the one that sent Chris Longo into town. It wasn't right that he could emerge unscathed from yet another crime, and one that ended in the murder of Barry Shy.

"They should take a look at him in the States, just in case," Dana told Benny.

"Not sure how much traction you would get. The books weren't stolen, and even if they were, that's a jurisdiction headache that would need to be resolved between the two countries."

"I would think it's something the FBI would be interested in. Who knows what other shenanigans he's wrapped up in."

"I feel you would be poking a bear, Dana. The best thing is to make sure you don't give Greyson Bay any reason to come after you."

Dana spent the rest of the afternoon and evening at home in Casa Verde alone. She was a bit jumpy, thinking she was seeing Greyson Bay around every corner of the house.

Although she insisted that Benny didn't have to come down to Mariposa Azul Beach, she was excited as he drove up the driveway and parked by her carport.

Benny arrived with a gym bag with a change of clothing and asked Dana if he could stay the night in the guest room.

"You don't have to stay here. I'll be fine, and I have Ramón keeping his eyes peeled."

"I know, but it will make me feel better if I stick around here for a night or two versus being at my beach house wondering if he was coming for those books."

"If Greyson is involved, he's probably not here running around. He sends his crook to do his dirty business. I'm sure he's still in New York. But thank you, because I won't lie, I am feeling a bit jumpy here by myself with him still out there."

They decided that even though it was late, that Dana should call Detective Rojas on her mobile phone to let her know about everything she had found out about Chris Longo's custom-order burglary business and that one of his clients, Greyson Bay, was the man she was using to appraise her collection of first-edition print books.

"Did she seem interested?" Benny asked after Dana hung up the phone.

"Yes, but she needs to discuss it with Picado in the morning, so who knows if they'll do anything more with it. She said the fact that Greyson is in the States means there is nothing they can do about it. And that his name hasn't come up at all during their investigation."

"He's set it up so he's like the Teflon Don and nothing sticks to him," Benny said.

"She was being honest with you, and she doubts Picado will authorize doing much about this since the case is closed. Chris Longo broke into your store to rob it. Barry Shy walked in on it, so he kills him. Then he was killed in a mugging gone bad while cavorting in the dangerous red light district zone before leaving the country, so Picado views it as karma meting out justice. Case closed." Benny shrugged, not finding much fault with his line of thinking.

Dana suggested she should just call Greyson Bay. "Put him on the spot. Ask him flat out."

"Remember what I said about poking bears? If he's really mixed up in all this, perhaps it's best not to show our hand and let him know that we have our suspicions about him. We'll call the FBI liaison office in the morning and let them look into it. So we'll have the OIJ and the FBI aware of it. We've done our part as citizens. Let the professionals handle it."

Dana sighed.

"I know you're right, but it's frustrating. I just want to hear his voice. Does he sound the same, or does he sound like he's worried or scared?"

"Well, it's almost one in the morning in New York, so at least sleep on it."

The next morning, Dana and Benny drove to the Qué Vista for breakfast. It was early, so it was just them and a tourist couple from Germany and two members of the Gossip Brigade, Doña Chilla and Doña Marta. The other two members, Doña Amada and Doña Luz, were not morning people.

They chatted briefly with the tourists. They were heading back to Germany the following day. Then they chatted up the old ladies.

"Good morning, young ladies," Benny said. He was met with laughter.

"Aren't you the charmer," Doña Chilla said.

"He's a lawyer, fake flattery must be part of the curriculum that they teach in law school," Doña Marta said tartly.

"Come on now," he said, smiling.

"Be thankful she spared you one of her lawyer jokes," Doña Chilla said.

Doña Marta cleared her throat and grinned. "That reminds me... do you know how many lawyer jokes are in existence?"

"Three. All the rest are true stories," Benny said, beating her to the punch line.

"You're no fun," Doña Marta said.

"They teach us all the lawyer jokes in law school too," Benny said with a wink as Doña Marta shooed him away like a fly and Doña Chilla laughed out loud.

Dana was amazed how being warm and personal seemed to come effortlessly to him. Dana was an introvert who had to make an effort to get to fifty percent of Benny's outgoing personality. She stood there watching the banter with a smile on her face when Doña Chilla turned to her.

"How are you doing, honey? You must be awfully excited to

have your bookstore open and that the awful man who killed Barry is dead."

"I'm excited and a little worried about starting a new business under such dark clouds," Dana said.

"Well, I'll be there when it's open, dear."

"Me too," Doña Marta added. That was nice of them. Two customers on opening day. Better than none. Dana smiled and thanked them.

Dana and Benny had breakfast. Benny had scrambled eggs, ham, plátanos maduros, and gallo pinto, while Dana opted for banana pancakes.

They ate silently, watching the waves drift in and out on the sand from the restaurant's deck. The warm air was sizzling, already serving as a harbinger of the heat that was to come later on in the day at full force.

THIRTY-TWO

After breakfast, Benny dropped off Dana at Casa Verde. They chitchatted a bit with Ramón, who was working on his new landscaping project by the front gate.

"Oh, those are beautiful flowers," Dana cooed.

Ramón was going to transform that lonely patch of grass into a beautiful tropical flower bed which would be one of the first things visitors see when they drove onto the property.

They talked a while about the flowers and his plans for the patch, then she turned to more serious matters. She filled him in on what was going on with the possibility that Chris Longo might have had an accomplice who was still out there on the loose.

"This other man is in the States, so I doubt he'll risk coming into the country to try to steal those books or hurt me. He's not that dumb or greedy," Dana explained to Ramón, who seemed concerned for her safety.

"That being said, it just makes sense for all of us to keep our eyes and ears open for the next few weeks," Benny added.

"I will, Don Benny," Ramón said, smiling wide and holding up his razor-sharp machete.

Dana laughed nervously. Benny gave him a big thumbs up.

"Ramón thinks he's a Roman legionnaire or something," Dana said as she and Benny walked side by side towards the main house.

"As you've seen, the campesinos are handy with a machete. There have been many reports of campesinos, drunk on Cacique Guaro, turning a drunkard bar brawl into a gladiator battle with their machetes."

Dana looked at him wide-eyed. "You must be kidding."

"Nope, I'm serious. It happens from time to time in the rural areas," Benny said, holding his hand up in the air as if he was being sworn in to testify in a court of law. "But don't worry, Ramón doesn't even drink. But, like Mr. T would say, I pity the fool that breaks into Casa Verde and tries to do you harm. I'm sure Ramón would slice him up like ham in a deli."

"Gross," Dana said, stifling a smile.

"Besides, I have my own equalizer," Benny said, pulling a case from his gym bag. He opened it to show her his pistol.

Guns made Dana nervous. She had read somewhere that the odds were greater of the assailant turning the tables and shooting the victim with their own gun than the other way around.

"Those make me nervous," Dana said.

"Nothing to it if you know how to use one. It's just a tool, like a hammer."

Dana shrugged. She had a machete-wielding Ramón outside of the home and a pistol-packing Benny and claw-packing Wally indoors, protecting her. If Greyson Bay was really behind everything and he was dumb enough to try and hurt her, he would probably regret that decision right quick.

Since Benny was supposed to be in the city, he had several back-to-back calls that he had to make for work, and he also needed to grab some documents he had left at his beach house, so he told her he would be back in a couple hours, since he was planning to spend the night in the guest room until the whole Greyson Bay situation was figured out.

"Don't worry, I'm fine. It's broad daylight, and I have Ramón and his machete outside and Wally and his claws inside."

Benny smiled and left, promising to be back in two hours tops.

Dana went to her study to start working on some new marketing materials for the new grand opening of the bookstore, since all other marketing stuff had an opening date that had come and gone.

Wally strutted his way into the study. He looked up at her on the computer and meowed loudly, stretching and yawning. He then rubbed up against her legs. "Good kitty," Dana said absentmindedly without even looking at the cat as she typed away on her laptop.

Wally wasn't one to be ignored. He jumped up on the desk in one move, startling Dana. "Dang you, Wally, you're going to give me a heart attack doing that."

He shoved his head into her hand and meowed. Dana was sure he just said something along the line of, *Don't care. Pet me, now.* So Dana did as he instructed.

She had set up a playlist of old-school Miami Sound Machine. Before Gloria Estefan became *the* Gloria Estefan singing about conga, she was a member of Miami Sound Machine, singing beautiful Spanish ballads that reminded Dana of The Carpenters.

The music set, she began to tap away on her computer as Wally demanded more attention. After a few minutes, she sat back to look at the graphic she had been working on. The text read GRAND REOPENING.

Then it dawned on her that there was never a grand opening, since the bookstore was never open and closed for a grand reopening. She deleted RE and added NEW. She looked at the flyer: NEW OPENING. *Better*, she thought. Wally meowed in agreement.

The bulk of the work for the opening had already been done. She just needed to update the materials.

She had been at it for almost two hours when her phone rang. She picked it up and looked at the display. She saw the 650 area code. It was Bucky. She leaped for the phone, causing Wally to scamper away.

"Sorry, Wally," she said, grabbing her phone from her desk. "Hey, Bucky."

"Are you at home?" There was an edge to his voice that made the hairs on Dana's arms stand straight up.

"Yes, why?"

"Are you alone?" Again, the tone of his voice was so unlike Bucky. The usually happy-go-lucky forty-year-old going on twenty sounded scared.

"No, well, kind of. What's up?"

"Sorry, I'll explain in a sec, but what do you mean, *kind of?*"

"I'm alone in the main house right now, but my caretaker, Ramón, lives in his own house on the property with his wife, Carmen. And Benny had to leave for work for a couple hours, but he'll be back and he's staying here in the guest room until we get this all sorted out. You're freaking me out, Bucky."

"Sorry, it's just, well..."

"Bucky, just say it!"

"I threw all the emails from Greyson Bay that you forwarded to me into my custom grinder to look for clues, any additional information that might not be clear looking at an email as a regular recipient."

"What did you find?"

"I looked at the data in the header of the emails, which is hidden."

Dana knew all about email headers. The metadata was tucked away, and most email-reading programs required the person to click on a button to reveal that hidden information.

"As I'm sure you know, there is a lot of useful stuff in there, like the routing information of all emails including the sender, recipient, and date, but the part of the header I'm most interested in is the part that provides information on the route an email takes as it is transferred from one computer to another. Following?"

"Yes, got it."

"So I opened his emails in my analyzer. The first emails you had received from Greyson Bay, when you first began to chat about the books, the IP address that was stamped in Greyson's email headers was from the borough of Manhattan in New York City, which makes sense, since that's where he lives. But the last few emails you received from Greyson, the IP address is not from New York City—it's from Costa Rica."

"What?" Dana could feel the blood draining from her. She felt lightheaded.

"He was sending those emails to you from Costa Rica. From an IP address in the Guanacaste Province in Nosara, which I googled, and is not far from where you live."

"That's about twenty minutes from Mariposa Beach," Dana said nervously. "Are you sure you're not looking at my IP address or something?" Dana knew right away that was a dumb question. There was no way Bucky had looked at the data wrong. It would be like a mathematician getting 2+2 wrong.

"I'm one thousand percent sure, girl. It's been eighty-four hours since the last email from Greyson, so he could be back to the States by now, but you need to be very careful, because what the heck was he doing down there, right? I'm assuming he never shared that little tidbit of information with you."

"No. On the contrary, he made it a point to tell me he was in his bookstore in New York."

"Well, he's lying. Why would he do that?"

"That confirms what we've been thinking. He wants my first editions. I was thinking he had sent Chris Longo to do the dirty work while he stayed in New York, but he must have actually traveled down here with him."

"And the only man that could point the finger in his direction was conveniently killed in a mugging gone bad," Bucky said.

"My left foot that was a mugging gone bad. He's probably behind that too," Dana said.

"You need to call nine-one-one. Do they have that there?"

"Yes, it's also nine-one-one here," Dana said, as if in a fog.

"Well, hang up and call the police."

Dana sat there for a moment, stunned. She dug around her purse and pulled out Detective Gabriela Rojas's business card. She looked at it. She figured she would call her directly than mess around with 911, since she had no idea how well it worked, especially being in secluded and tiny Mariposa Beach.

Rojas picked up after two rings. Dana told her everything Bucky had shared about Greyson Bay being in Costa Rica and about how he knew the value of her first-edition books down to the penny.

"Okay, let me take a look to see if he's entered the country and more importantly, if he has left. Stay put in your house. You have that secured wall and front gate, so you should be safe in there. Let Ramón know what's up, but call him. I don't want you to leave your house until I figure out what's going on with this Greyson Bay character."

Dana felt a sense of calm after hanging up the phone. The

detective sounded calm, confident, and in charge. But there was the fact that she was over an hour away in Nicoya. And Officer Freddy was twenty minutes away.

Dana called Benny next. She got his voicemail. *Drat*, he had told her he was going to be in those back-to-back calls. She left him a voicemail with the latest developments.

Next, she called Ramón on his mobile phone, which she knew he always kept in his pocket. He picked up and she told him what was going on.

"Don't worry, Doña Dana, if anyone tries to sneak onto the property, I'll know."

She liked that he sounded confident, but how could he be so sure? Casa Verde sat on 120 acres of property that couldn't be watched by one man.

Maybe Greyson Bay had already gotten onto her property and was now just waiting for the perfect opportunity to pounce. And he didn't know about Bucky and Benny and that the police knew about him. He might still believe that by killing her, she would be the last link to him.

She sat down, scared. She wished she had accepted Benny's offer to leave his gun with her. "Oh, I'll probably just shoot my foot with it," she had joked.

"Breathe deep. Relax," she began her relaxation technique. It worked well when she was stressed with work or dealing with an annoying coworker, or when she would argue with her ex-husband, but it wasn't working too well in calming her down with the notion that Greyson Bay was in Costa Rica and could be coming after her.

THIRTY-THREE

It had been fifteen minutes since she got off the phone with Bucky. And the more she thought about it, the less likely she thought that Greyson Bay was still in town. She felt goofy for freaking out so badly.

She went upstairs to wait for Benny and Rojas to call her back. She felt safer upstairs in her veranda, overlooking her property from above, sitting on her favorite chair.

She saw Ramón down below. He seemed to be standing on guard. She smiled, feeling safer.

She sat down and put the hiking stick she had grabbed to serve as a weapon just in case down on the table.

She had her laptop with her. She thought about reading a book or a magazine online, but her nerves were too much on edge to focus on reading. She did nothing but look out at her property and glance at the phone, hoping Benny would call her back.

After a few minutes, her phone trilled, announcing the arrival of a text message. She looked at her phone. It was from Benny:

On my way

She felt a relief. She always prided herself on being fiercely independent, even when she was married. It was one of the things that had affected her marriage. Her ex-husband wanted a more needy, wallflower-type wife. It was two things she never was and wasn't keen to be, even when they had met in college; why he thought she would change, she would never know, but then again, she should have known Phil's overbearing personality wasn't going to change, either. Nuggets of information two twenty-year-olds in love chose to ignore.

But finding out that someone you thought you could trust might be behind the murder of Barry Shy, all over books? It seemed crazy to her. But she knew people had been killed for far less.

Dana was lost in thought when her phone rang, startling her. It was Detective Rojas. Dana anxiously answered it.

"I have confirmed that Greyson Bay entered Costa Rica via the Juan Santamaría Airport ten days ago and there is no exit stamp, so he's still in the country. He flew in from Atlanta on the same flight with Chris Longo."

"Oh, jeez," Dana said, glancing over at her hiking stick.

"Yes, not good. Listen, Dana. I'm mobilizing a SERT team to your house." SERT was the equivalent to a SWAT team in the United States. "Unfortunately, the fastest I can get a SERT team mobilized down to Mariposa Beach is in forty-five minutes. Agent Picado and I are on our way down from Nicoya too, and I have Officer Freddy Sanchez on his way from Guiones Beach, so he'll be the first police presence to arrive. Until then, stay put in your house. Do not leave your property, okay?"

"Yes, okay," Dana said, sounding lightheaded.

"I have an all-points-bulletin out for his arrest with the entire police force from the transit police, municipal police, and customs at the airport and in the border with Nicaragua and

Panama, so if tries to sneak out of the country, he will be caught. So hang in there. We'll get the son of a gun."

Dana stood from the chair and leaned on the railing of her deck. She saw Ramón walking down the driveway towards the front gate.

She was just going to ask him to man the front gate, so she was relieved to see him heading that way. She watched him for about a minute before he was out of sight. She could not see the front gate from anywhere in her house.

She sat back down and fired up the security camera she had mounted on the front gate. She pulled up the crisp high-definition video feed, which offered a wide view, and saw everything was quiet out there.

She then thought about the back and how that was the weak spot from a security perspective and exactly how Chris Longo had broken into her bookstore.

She was comforted that the entire property was surrounded by a tall concrete wall with jagged pieces of broken glass embedded into the cement at the top, making it very difficult for anyone to not just reach the top of the wall, but also to climb over it without getting cut up.

It was standard security seen in most homes in Costa Rica. Jarring at first for the new expat or the tourists, but then you got used to it, and on that day, Dana was over the moon happy her uncle had secured Casa Verde so well. But it's not like she was living in Fort Knox, and Casa Verde sat on 120 acres of land, so a determined person could make it over the wall undetected somewhere along the property.

Wally meowed just then. "Okay, sure, you'll protect me," Dana said to him as she rubbed his chin. She was still rubbing his chin when a new text from Benny arrived. It simply stated: *at the gate.*

Dana was overjoyed as she looked at the 9-inch high-resolution color LCD screen monitor and saw Benny's white Land Cruiser driving in.

Ramón must have let him in as he usually did. She watched the monitor to make sure no one was lurking around, trying to piggyback behind him, and by anyone, she meant Greyson Bay.

The monitor indicated the gate was shut, and she didn't see any suspicious activity. Feeling relieved, she headed downstairs and opened the front door to greet Benny. She felt bad tearing him away from his law practice but was happy he was there to keep her company until the police began to arrive. She was so freaked out, she was even looking forward for Detective Picado to show up, scowling as usual.

The driveway leading from the front gate to the main house was one-quarter of a mile long, so she could hear Benny's truck crunching on the gravel before she could actually see it.

She came downstairs and opened the front door to greet him. She smiled when she saw the familiar white SUV drive up towards the front of the house. He parked by the carport as usual.

She could see him sitting on the driver's side, seemingly talking to someone. She looked closer and she could see fear in his face. He looked up and they made eye contact. His face was ashen. That's when she heard Benny scream in a blood-curdling manner she had never heard from him before, "Run back inside."

THIRTY-FOUR

After Benny yelled, she noticed for the first time that someone was in the back seat right behind him. She saw that person's arm go up in the air above Benny's head. The person was holding something in his hand. She was too far away to see what it was, and what happened was clear as the man in the backseat brought his arm down hard, striking Benny in the back of the head so hard with the object that she heard a loud *thwack* that sounded like someone had hit a melon with a hammer.

"No!" Dana screamed without even realizing she had opened her mouth.

She watched Benny slump forward and a gloved hand shoving him to the side.

Everything seemed to be happening in slow motion as far as Dana could tell. The backseat door on the driver's side was flung open, and Greyson Bay jumped out, holding a black gun in his right hand.

Greyson Bay looked at her and smiled, but there was murder in his eyes.

"At last, we meet in person," he said sinisterly. "Don't you move, Dana," Bay said, pointing the gun at her.

She had no idea what came over her. It was as if she was having an out-of-body experience, but she ran back inside, slamming the door shut. She heard the sound of the gunshot and heard it striking the wooden door.

She screamed and quickly turned the lever to the deadbolt, and she ran upstairs. She heard banging at the door, so she ran up two steps at a time. She tripped at the top, banging her knee hard on the hard tile. She hissed and watched in amazement as her knee ballooned in size right in front of her eyes.

"Get up," she yelled at herself. She got to her feet and scampered all gimpy to her bedroom, then out the sliding doors to her deck. She grabbed the hiking stick and felt dumb about bringing a hiking stick to a gunfight, but it was better than nothing.

"The police are on their way, Greyson, including a SWAT team, no lie, so just leave right now," Dana shouted from the entryway of the patio doors leading from her bedroom to the veranda. She wanted to peer over her railing down below, but wasn't about to give him a clear shot. She could hear him banging on the door, and from a crack on her wood deck, she could see him down below, pacing around frantically like a bull at a gate.

"Give me those books and I'll leave."

"Oh, brother, you can't really be that much of a numbskull. I don't have those books here or in the bookstore. I gave them to my lawyer for safekeeping. They're stored safely in a bank vault in San José. You went through all this. You took a man's life for nothing. For books that are five hours away, protected inside a bank that you'll never get access to. Just go before the police arrive."

"I didn't kill that busybody hippy. That was Chris's doing. Not that I blame him. He told me what happened. How he was just making sure you didn't have the books hidden in your store. He wanted to check there first, since it was easy pickings for him to break into your store in comparison to this fortress you're living in here. So he breaks in and was searching your place when that idiot confronted him for breaking and entering. Starts ranting and raving about thievery, and that Jerry Garcia look-alike takes out an old Polaroid camera. An honest-to-goodness old-school Polaroid camera because he's too Zen for digital, I guess. So he's going to take Chris's picture and he's going to make copies and plaster them all over the province. Well, he couldn't let that happen, so he had to kill him."

"I'm not lying about the police, Greyson, they're on the way here as we speak. Just go."

"I believe you. But it will take them a while to get to this lovely little beach town tucked away in the middle of nowhere. I've done my homework."

"I already told you, I don't have the books."

"Maybe I just kill you, your stupid boyfriend, and that idiot peasant at the front gate. Just for messing up all my plans."

Dana actually felt relief, since that meant that Benny and Ramón must still be alive, and she hoped that if Carmen was aware of what was happening, that she had the good sense to not leave the safety of her house.

"You said you're not a killer. Why start now, over nothing?"

He laughed, and it was the creepiest laugh she had ever heard, like the demented Joker. Guttural. Evil. Frightening.

"I said I didn't kill that moron in your bookstore. But who do you think killed idiot Chris?"

Dana didn't say a word. She didn't dare. Let him confess to everything. She hit the record button on her phone.

"Yeah, that's right. Chris wanted to run away back to the States. Mister Tough Guy was a ball of nerves, acting like a cat dunked in water. I had him meet me in the seediest part of town. So I popped him with this here local pistol I bought off some meth head on the streets," Greyson said as he waved the gun in his hand in the air like it was show-and-tell.

"That way the police would think it was a local junkie that killed him. A mugging gone bad. Case closed. Then I could sneak back down here to get what I came all this way for... those books!"

"Your plan worked, so just go," Dana pleaded.

"Yeah, but that's all over now. You told the police. Your boyfriend. I'm sure the whole town knows about me by now, so this isn't about the books anymore, it's about your snooping and not leaving well enough alone. You ruined my life, so I'm going to take yours," Bay seethed.

Dana could see him through the crack in the floor as he raised his arm, aiming the gun up towards her. She dove into her bedroom as three shots ripped into the deck mere inches from where she had been standing. Chunks of wood splinters flew through the air. Dana hid under her bed.

She heard the sound of feet crunching on the gravel and then she heard the sound of the car door opening. *Thank goodness he's leaving*, Dana thought.

"Oh, Dana," she heard Bay say mockingly.

She looked out her bedroom window down below and was horrified at what she saw. Greyson had dragged an unconscious Benny from the SUV and had laid him out on the ground. In front of his truck. Bay stood over him, pointing the gun at Benny.

"No, don't do it, Greyson, are you crazy?" Dana shouted as she ran out towards the edge of the deck. She could see the bullet holes, which made her tremble.

"Looks like we have ourselves our own Costa Rican stand-off," he said, laughing. "I might as well go out like in *Butch Cassidy and the Sundance Kid* versus rotting away in a Costa Rican jail."

Dana felt the tears coming down her cheeks.

It felt like she stood there for hours, but it was mere seconds when all of a sudden Benny came to and he groggily reached for Greyson's legs, causing him to lose his footing and he fell down to the ground next to Benny and they began to wrestle, kicking up dust and gravel from the driveway.

Dana saw Bay's gun skittering down the driveway. Without even thinking, she ran back downstairs, pushing away the pain she felt in her knee for the moment. She unlocked the door and stumbled outside, almost falling again, but she kept her balance as she ran towards Bay's gun and picked it up. She tried to aim the gun at Bay, but he and Benny were intertwined like two Greco-Roman wrestlers on the mat.

She screamed for Greyson to stop, but at that moment he managed to get the upper hand on Benny, who seemed dazed from the blow to the head he had suffered. Suddenly Greyson was on top of Benny, and he grabbed him by his hair and slammed the back of his head onto the driveway, knocking him out cold again. He was going to do that again when Dana screamed as she held the gun on him.

"Don't you do it, or I'll shoot."

Greyson stopped, seeming to just realize that Dana was there and that she was pointing his gun at him.

He looked at Dana. He was sweating and was covered in dust, gravel, and blood. He breathed out heavily as he let go of Benny's head and rolled off him. He was sitting on the ground, heaving, out of breath.

"Do you like to gamble, Dana?" he finally said after catching his breath.

"We're not playing twenty questions here, Greyson. I don't want to shoot you, but I will if you force me to. So just sit there until the police arrive."

"I like to gamble. And I bet that you don't have the guts to pull that trigger," he said, studying her face.

"I wouldn't make that bet," Dana said. She tried to sound tough, but her shaky hand was showing the poor hand she was holding. She always did have a terrible poker face.

He smiled. "Okay, okay," he said, putting his hands in the air. "Don't shoot."

"Don't move and I won't."

Greyson had his knees up to his chest and his hands on the ground. "You got it," he said, when suddenly both his hands came up from the ground, where he had grabbed two fistfuls of gravel and dirt from the ground, and he threw them at Dana's face. She flinched and ducked down, most of the gravel missing her, but a few of the loose pebbles and a swath of dirt hit her on the lower part of the face. She must have been shouting, because she felt dirt and gravel in her mouth, causing her to choke and cough.

By the time Dana recovered, Greyson had leapt to his feet and was bum-rushing her. Dana closed her eyes and pulled the trigger. She opened them and saw dirt fly in the air next to Greyson. She missed, and he didn't flinch. He almost had her in his grasp when she fired one more time. This time, she didn't close her eyes.

She took two steps back and watched him jump on one foot and yelled, "You shot me! I can't believe you shot me!"

"I told you not to make that bet," Dana said, sounding all tough. She felt like Dirty Harry.

Greyson was still hopping. "You shot me in the foot," he said as he fell to the ground. He sat up on the ground, holding his foot and crying and whimpering about how she shot him.

"You're lucky I have terrible aim and shot you in the foot, unlike how you killed Chris Longo," Dana said, holding the gun with both hands as she pointed it at him.

"I have more bullets, so don't push your luck. This isn't *Butch Cassidy and the Sundance Kid*," Dana said, sounding even more confident as she stood over him.

THIRTY-FIVE

Dana stood over Greyson Bay, white-knuckling the gun she kept pointed at him for hours. Well, it felt like hours to her. It was really less than five minutes when Officer Freddy Sanchez came blazing in on his motocross motorcycle. Carmen had emerged from hiding in her house in tears and she opened the front gate to let Officer Freddy inside. He looked shocked, seeing how Dana had subdued Greyson Bay on her own.

"I didn't have a choice but to shoot him," a shell-shocked Dana said as Greyson writhed on his back in the ground in pain.

"It's okay," Freddy said as he flipped Greyson over onto his stomach and in one motion he handcuffed him to his back. Greyson protested that the handcuffs were too tight and how much his foot hurt. Freddy told him to shut up.

Freddy turned to Dana and asked if she was all right.

Dana couldn't speak, so she nodded as tears welled up in her eyes again, and she began to shake as the adrenaline began to drain from her body.

Freddy carefully took the gun from Dana's death grip. "It's okay, give me the gun," he told her gently as she finally released her grip.

"I need to see a doctor, man," Greyson whined. He was now facedown in the dirt.

"There are several ambulances on the way," Freddy said as he looked at Greyson's foot.

"I'm dying here, man."

"Oh, please, she shot you in the foot, in and out, you'll live. But you are very much under arrest," Officer Freddy said.

He put on a latex glove and put the gun into an evidence bag. He looked at the evidence and smiled. "Well, well, well, looks like the same kind of gun that killed your accomplice, Chris Longo."

Greyson breathed out heavily, causing dust and dirt to fly into the air and into his mouth. He coughed and begged to be let up.

"The OIJ will be here soon, as well as the ambulance. Until then, you're just fine right there in the dirt," Freddy said.

He joined Dana, who had recovered and was tending to Benny. Freddy looked at him and opened his eyes with his thumb and index finger. Then he felt for his pulse. "Looks like he has a concussion. A nasty one from the looks of things, but his breathing and pulse seem fine to me, so I think he'll be okay. He'll have a pretty nasty headache, but in the scheme of things, that's not too bad," Freddy said.

"Thank God, I thought he killed him. He hit him over the head with the gun, then he slammed the back of his head on the ground," Dana explained.

"Better not touch anything until the OIJ and the forensics team get here," Freddy said as he walked over to his motorcycle and removed a big roll of yellow crime scene tape.

A few minutes later, Carmen came walking up the driveway with her arms wrapped around Ramón, who was waking next to her slowly, as if he had just woken up from a drunken stupor.

Dana watched as Ramón looked around, seeing Freddy

corner off the crime scene. He turned red with anger when he saw the handcuffed Greyson Bay on the floor.

"That son of a gun," he seethed at Greyson in Spanish.

"Are you okay, Ramón?" Dana asked as she got up from Benny's side and walked towards Ramón and Carmen.

"I'm fine. I'm so sorry, Doña Dana, I thought it was just Don Benny in his car, so I let him in and then suddenly this man attacked me, and the next thing I remember, I wake up and look up at Carmen, who was kneeling beside me, shaking me." He smiled, looking at his wife with love in his eyes.

"I thought you were dead," she said, hugging her husband tight.

Freddy walked over to Ramón and took a look at his head. "Looks like you'll be joining the concussion club along with Benny," he said with a smile. "But hey, at least he hit you with the gun, and didn't shoot you. Lucky guys, you two."

Greyson Bay began to scream again about how tight the handcuffs were and how he had dirt in his mouth and how his foot hurt. Freddy, Ramón, and Dana all replied in almost unison, "Shut up."

They were all laughing as Benny began to come out of it. Dana knelt back down next to him, then she shuddered in pain. "You need to put some ice on that knee," Officer Freddy said, looking at the swollen knee. "How did that happen?"

"I fell," Dana said, sounding embarrassed. But she didn't care about her knee just then. She just looked down at Benny and smiled as his eyes fluttered a bit, and suddenly he was back. He tried to sit too fast, and he winced in pain, holding his head.

"Take it easy," Dana said. "You got hit in the head pretty bad. You got knocked out, twice."

"A lot of help I was in protecting you," Benny said, sitting up. He ran his fingers through his head, finding two big lumps in the back. "Ouch," he said.

Dana smiled. "It all worked out, so that doesn't matter now."

She felt proud, though. Her two protectors, Benny and Ramón, armed with a handgun and a machete, and she ended up saving them all, having started out with just a hiking sick for a weapon.

EPILOGUE

Two weeks later.

Mariposa Books, the first bookstore in the history of Mariposa Beach, finally opened for business. The grand opening was a few weeks behind schedule, but better late than never, Dana thought as she looked around at her jam-packed open house.

It seemed everyone from town had joined the celebration. The Gossip Brigade ladies were there, whispering and gossiping about who knows what.

Big Mike was perusing the travel section, looking through *The Surfer's Guide to Costa Rica* as he munched on one of Mindy's banana walnut muffins.

Mindy was manning the refreshments and treats corner. She refused to accept a dime from Dana. "My treat," she told her, and Dana insisted on paying for the delicious muffins, tres leches cake, and the coffee and tea she provided to those in attendance.

Detective Gabriela Rojas and Officer Freddy Sanchez were there. Detective Picado was a no-show, which really didn't surprise Dana, and that was fine with her.

She had actually been surprised on the day that Greyson Bay had been arrested that Picado had grunted half an apology for leaving her to fend a homicidal nut case on her own.

Ramón and Carmen were at the grand opening, smiling and helping Dana out even though she insisted they were there as guests only. Ramón had a scar and bruise on his forehead that served as a visible reminder of Greyson Bay's dastardly deeds in town on that day, and all just for greed. He wanted the money that Dana's valuable book collection would have generated.

Their son, Claudio was there, too. He told Dana he was excited to start his new job at the Four Seasons the following week. Gustavo Barca was not happy with the defection, and even threatened to sue over some non-compete clause nonsense. Benny promised to represent him pro bono if Barca dared to proceed with it.

Benny's hair was shaved off, and he looked like a soldier at boot camp. His head injury from Bay pistol-whipping him required some stitches, so the doctor had to shave a chunk of his back hair to mend him up from Greyson's brutal assault. Benny decided to shave all his brown hair off versus having an odd-looking mismatch.

"You have the Three Stooges' Curly haircut," Dana teased him.

He was standing next to Dana, taking in the excitement of the grand opening with her.

He was still struggling with the symptoms of the concussion, which made Dana feel terrible. But he would remind her, "If it wasn't for you, I would be six feet under, so thank you. I can deal with the concussion much better than the alternative of having no symptoms because I'm dead and buried."

"Everything looks so great, babe," Courtney said.

"Yeah, just awesome," Bucky added.

"I'm glad you two can be part of this, sort of," Dana said, talking into her iPad.

"It's like we're there," Courtney said via video chat. Bucky had driven up from Palo Alto and was hanging out with Courtney in San Francisco so they could be part of her big day via video. They all laughed like they were in the same room together instead of being close to four thousand miles apart as Dana walked around with her iPad so her two Bay Area friends could take it all in.

Greyson Bay was taken into custody by the OIJ and charged with the murder of Chris Longo and as an accessory to the murder of Barry Shy, as well as with the attempted murder of Ramón Villalobos, Benny Campos, and Dana Kirkpatrick. He was imprisoned at the notorious San Sebastián prison under preventive detention where prisoners who have yet to be convicted are sent if a judge believes they are a flight risk.

"He better get used to our prison system, because he's going to be a part of it for many decades," Rojas had said to Dana.

Dana was just glad it was all over.

"What about that couple you were suspicious about?" Courtney asked.

"I guess I was just being paranoid," Dana said laughing.

"How are things with Benny?" Courtney asked. Dana could see Bucky smiling wide next to Courtney.

Dana smiled. "It's good."

She and Benny had become even closer after what they had gone through.

Benny's doctor had recommended that he take it easy for a few weeks while he recovered from the serious concussion he had received. "You need to relax and take it easy," the doctor had told him.

Benny had told Dana that there wasn't anywhere he felt

more relaxed than at his beach house in Mariposa Beach and spending time with her.

She had blushed with a smile. She was sad about the injury but happy he would be spending the next few weeks in town.

It had been a rocky start to her bookstore, but finally she was in business. She looked around proudly. It was her first business, and she couldn't be happier than running a bookstore in Mariposa Beach.

SNEAK PEEK: A REALITY SHOW TO DIE FOR

Here is an exclusive sneak peek at *A Reality Show To Die For* (the third book in the Costa Rica Beach Cozy Mystery series).

Chapter One

The day that Hollywood came to the tiny beach town of Mariposa Beach in Costa Rica had started out like any other day at the Books, Bagels, and Lattes bookstore cafe.

As usual, the cafe got busy with the early-morning rush-hour crowd of caffeine-deprived and hungry locals and tourists, but by late morning the crowd dissipated until the lunch rush.

On that day, the sound of rumbling engines made the windows of the bookstore cafe rattle, disrupting the quiet. Dana Kirkpatrick and her friend and new business partner, Mindy Salas, looked at each other with wonderment in their eyes as they both rushed to the front window to look outside to see what causing the noise.

They saw several large buses lumbering into town.

Mindy's husband, Leo, had also heard the noise, so he had popped his head from the back kitchen. "Oh boy, here we go," he said ominously.

"They're here," Mindy said, saying it like the little girl from the *Poltergeist* movie did.

Even Wally, Dana's shorthaired white cat and whom Dana had anointed the official bookstore cat, had jumped up by the windowsill to watch the excitement unfolding outside.

"Wow, those buses are over the top," Dana said, looking at the large luxury buses pulling into town.

"It's the same buses that rock stars ride along in," Mindy said, sounding impressed as Amalfi Soto joined them at the window.

To Dana, they looked like two large, gaudy billboards on wheels. They had wrapped every inch of the buses with an advertisement for the hit reality television show, *The Island*.

The logo of the show was an island with palm trees and several stickmen in athletic poses like Olympians, and they had wrapped the entire buses with the show's logo and the headshot of the show's longtime host, Chris Day. His smiling face covered the entire center panels of the buses from the side flap to the roof — including the windows.

"Oh Lordy, that's one creepy man right there," Dana said, chuckling.

"That's the host of the show, he is so handsome." Mindy smiled wistfully as she spoke to Dana, but her gaze was on the bus.

"Hey, now," her husband said, pretending to be jealous.

Amalfi Soto, who worked for Dana, seemed in a trance looking out the window, and Dana didn't want to know what was going through her young nineteen-year-old mind because it was probably NSFW.

"That bus wrap is over the top, don't you think?" Dana asked.

"I think it looks cool," Amalfi said, focused on the scene outside.

"I think it's supposed to be over the top, silly," Mindy giggled.

Since they outnumbered Dana, she said nothing more, not wanting to be a Debbie Downer, since Mindy and Amalfi seemed to be fans of the show, Chris Day, and the bus decor.

Leo had already disappeared back into the kitchen.

Regardless of what she thought about the show or the buses, she was excited to have the beach town jam-packed with cast and crewmembers ready to spend some money on books, coffee, and bagels.

Especially coming within the month since Dana and Mindy had combined their businesses—Dana's bookstore, and Mindy's cafe—under the same roof.

The idea to combine the businesses had come when Mindy's landlord saw how successful the cafe had become over the years, so he stuck her with a 300 percent rent increase. He figured she wouldn't want to move. He figured wrong.

Dana had bought her retail property for her bookstore outright versus renting in the heart of Mariposa Beach's tiny business district, known as Ark Row, across the street from Mindy's cafe.

One evening when Mindy was stressing out about what she would do about the exorbitant rent increase, Dana had an epiphany. "Move your cafe into my bookstore."

Dana remembered Mindy looking at her like she was off her rocker.

"I'm serious. I have a lot of room. I try as hard as I can, but my bookstore still looks scarce. And it's not like they're lining out the door to buy a book compared to the lines I see forming outside your cafe every day. You can have half of my retail space, which will be larger than what you have now. I'll even knock off some of your rent, and I promise I'll never be a pain in the rear landlord, nor would I ever try to gouge you with rent increases. We keep the business receipts separate. What you make from your cafe is all yours and what I make from the bookstore side is mine, so that stays the same, although you would miss out on the very lucrative bookstore business," Dana said, laughing.

Mindy laughed loudly at that.

"Okay, okay, not that funny," Dana said teasingly. "Besides, books, bagels, and coffee go together like peanut butter and jelly," Dana added, finishing her pitch.

After discussing it with her husband, who did most of the baking and managed the kitchen, and after they looked at the space to see if the move would be possible, Mindy and Leo agreed to combine the two businesses. Mariposa Books and Mindy's Coffee and Bagels became Mariposa Books, Bagels, and Lattes.

The move had gone smoothly, but there were a few days where they had to close, and the moving expenses for the Salas were a tad over budget, so the show coming to town was a boon to the entire local economy during the usual slowness of the wet season in Costa Rica, but it seemed like a lifeline to the new bookstore slash cafe, as Dana liked to refer to the new arrangement.

Besides, it wasn't every day that their sleepy little beach town got the Hollywood treatment.

After eleven seasons, the show was a big money earner for the studio, so they kept on cranking it out season after season.

In true Hollywood fashion, the network executives would squeeze every last drop of that moneymaking lemon until they sucked it dry and tossed what remained into the compost bin.

Dana had read that it was dirt cheap to produce reality TV compared to a network drama or sitcom.

The cast was made up of unknowns eager for a shot at fifteen minutes of fame and the one-million-dollar grand prize for the last person left on *The Island*.

The production company shot the shows on exotic islands in places like Costa Rica, Thailand, The Philippines, Indonesia, and other spots around the globe that were considered dirt cheap to shoot on location compared to the cost of shooting in LA.

It would be the second time they filmed a season in Costa Rica. Although Costa Rica was not an island, the country had several small, sparsely populated, rugged islands off both of its coasts.

The producers had chosen the tiny island of Santa Rita, which was located about twenty miles from the shores of Mariposa Beach, which was nestled right into the Nicoya Peninsula Bay.

The Nicoya Peninsula was the largest peninsula in the country and home to some of the most isolated and beautiful beaches, which made it a popular tourist destination.

Dana figured the fact that they had a pier that had served as the launching point to the island for decades had been a big reason why the producers chose their town to service as their headquarters while they shot the show.

It was a big production, with hundreds of producers and crewmembers arriving in August, which was one of the wettest months of the year, which meant that the jungle would be lush and green but everything would be wet and muddy from the daily rain and blasts of torrential downpours—a plus for the show's producers.

The tourist industry took a hit during the wet season, which is why it's considered the off-season for tourism. That also meant that the prices of just about everything went way down, and vacancies at the hotels and Airbnb were plentiful. Dana figured that was another reason the production company liked to film their show in August. Not only did the rainy weather make getting around more challenging, with muddy landslides, choppy waters, and with nonstop wet rain beating down on the cast members, it also made for much more compelling television to watch than blue skies and sunshine.

For the locals, it was a welcomed boost to the economy during its slow season, so they were more than happy to have the production team choose Mariposa Beach as their headquarters. It surprised Dana that the municipal mayor of Nicoya and his cronies weren't there rolling out the red carpet to welcome the production company.

Dana wasn't around when the reality show came to town five years earlier, but everyone who had been there told her they would pack her bookstore slash cafe with cast and crewmembers and that she should brace herself.

She had moved to the small, quirky beach town from the bustling and congested San Francisco a few months ago. It was a nice change of pace. It hadn't been a smooth move to town—far from it.

She had inherited her uncle's beach house, much to the chagrin of her cousin and his wife. Things got messy, really messy. There was a lawsuit and a murder—town gossip had her pegged as the probable killer. It was not a good introduction to the community.

Everything worked out with the lawsuit squashed, the murder solved, and the beach house known as Casa Verde and the acres of land it was on were all hers.

She had settled in nicely since then and had become a business owner for the first time in her life. And now there was the excitement of the show coming to town.

Mindy had been in business in town for over a decade, so she was here when *The Island* first came to town, and she had confirmed what Dana had heard from the locals that the production team was like money in the bank.

The town merchants of Ark Row called the production team walking ATMs.

"It will get crazy busy and we will make a lot of money," Mindy squealed. "But a warning," she said, her voice going from excited to ominous, "the crew is wonderful, but the cast can be a nightmare. A bunch of prima donna mactors."

"What the heck is a mactor?" Dana asked.

She had lived in LA and thought she knew the entire industry lingo. Mindy smiled and explained, "Model slash actors equals mactors."

"Oh, brother," Dana said, rolling her eyes.

"You'll see for yourself, half of them think they're the next great actor or actress, like they're a young Robert DeNiro or Meryl Streep, while the other half fancy themselves as super-models like Gisele Bündchen or Cindy Crawford."

Dana laughed at Mindy's descriptions.

"Did you forget I'm from California? I'm used to dealing with that kind of crazy. And although Northern California is more chill when it comes to Hollywood fakery, I lived for several years in Los Angeles, where dealing with plastic people like that was the norm."

Dana jostled her brown hair and made duck lips for added emphasis as Mindy and Amalfi cracked up.

As soon as the bus doors parted, open people began to pile out in droves. Most were young... very young.

Dana, Mindy, and Amalfi continued to watch as the chaotic scene outside unfolded when suddenly they saw several of them pointing towards their shop, and a horde of them began to make their way over. "Leo, incoming!" Mindy shouted over her shoulder towards the kitchen.

"Showtime," he shouted back.

"I'm ready for my close-up, Mr. DeMille," Dana said, and she and Mindy started laughing hysterically.

Amalfi looked confused, not getting the reference to the old movie, which made Dana and Mindy laugh even louder, feeling their age.

Get your copy here!

https://kcames.com/reality

ABOUT K.C.

I was born and raised in Costa Rica, but now live in San Francisco, California. I've always loved cozy mysteries, so when I decided to write one, I just knew I had to base it in my home country of Costa Rica!

That's how this beach cozy mystery series came about. I'm excited to bring you more cozy mysteries set in the beautiful tropical Pacific Coast of Costa Rica.

You can learn more about me and my books over at my website: www.KCAmes.com.

Sign up for my newsletter for book updates, animal pics, and my recipe book of traditional Costa Rica dishes, for free:

kcames.com/subscribe

And join my reader group on Facebook to say hello and make new friends:

kcames.com/group

ALSO BY K.C. AMES

A Beach House To Die For

A Book To Die For

A Reality Show To Die For